holding out for Mr. Right

holding out for Mr. Right

a novel

J.K. BRANTLEY

TATE PUBLISHING & Enterprises

Published by Tate Publishing & Enterprises, LLC
127 E. Trade Center Terrace | Mustang, Oklahoma 73064 USA
1.888.361.9473 | www.tatepublishing.com

Tate Publishing is committed to excellence in the publishing industry. The company reflects the philosophy established by the founders, based on Psalm 68:11,
"The Lord gave the word and great was the company of those who published it."

Book design copyright © 2010 by Tate Publishing, LLC. All rights reserved.
Cover design by Kellie Southerland
Interior design by Jeff Fisher

Published in the United States of America

ISBN: 978-1-61663-394-3
1. Fiction, Christian, Romance
2. Fiction, Romance, Contemporary
11.01.19

Dedication

To the men who matter most in my life.

My husband, David, for his support, encouragement, and sanity when my head is in the clouds. For our love—even through the bumps of the day to day, our love is endless. For our family—thank you for blessing me with our children and for making us a priority. David, you are my everything, my best friend, companion, lover, and most of all my soul mate. I love you.

In memory of:

My grandfather, Everett, who showed me
everything about faith and salvation.

My dad, Ken, who was my hero. I
will always be his little girl.

My father-in-law, R.V., who loved
me like his own from day one.

M adison Trent tossed and turned as she tried to get the beeping noise inside her head to stop. Then clearing her mind, she realized that it was her alarm going off at her usual 6:00 A.M. Madison leaned over and hit snooze and closed her eyes, lying there. She just started to fall back asleep when the alarm went off again. This time the red numbers showed 6:30 A.M. Madison pushed back the covers and sat up slowly. She normally did not hit snooze, but she had been on dead-lines with her interior design business. The stress was starting to catch up with her. She threw the blankets off and swung her bare legs out of the bed as her toes sunk into the plush, ivory carpet. Standing, she reached for the worn out pink robe and walked absently into the kitchen. She glanced around, feeling her mind clearing, admiring her masterpiece as the coffee started.

Madison was a highly successful interior designer, who, for the last eight years, hit the world big. People from all over Texas were calling her office trying to get her to decorate their homes and offices. She giggled as she reached for a cup, filled it with coffee, and headed into her bathroom. Madison glanced at the big, deep tub, her first project on her own home, thinking of all of the important society leaders and millionaires who wanted her to decorate their homes and offices. She had over twenty employees who worked for her at Trent Design while she was out teaching conferences all over Texas, Oklahoma, Colorado, Nevada, and New Mexico. The clients didn't want her employees, they wanted her to decorate their spaces. She smiled as she stepped into the steamy shower. She had it all—great business, beautiful house, and a new Mercedes SUV sitting in her driveway.

She paused, thinking back into the past, and sighed. She had also known disappointment. Her parents had gotten a divorce when she was nine years old. She had thought her dad had hung the moon up until that point. She would never forget all that she went through during the divorce and after. Not to mention that in high school she had dated a not-so-great guy. But she knew that she was put on this earth for a reason and that God was completely in control.

She had attended church her whole life, but now in her mid-thirties, she wasn't as involved like she should be. Oh, and one more thing was missing: a significant other. She was too busy for the games and the complications of a relationship, plus she wanted someone who had the same beliefs and would go to church with her. Her grandfather had told her, "If a guy really likes you, he will go to church with you." That saying had stuck with Madison for all these years, and she was yet to find her Mr. Right. She also thought of herself as being a bit reserved. She was well liked, but at first, others thought of her as a bit snobby and unapproachable. She definitely held herself to a higher standard and wondered if anyone could fill those shoes. Somehow she seriously doubted it.

As she lathered up her long, blonde hair, Madison could not remember the last time that she went out on a date. She had dinner with men, yes, but they were all potential clients. They made the moves, but Madison had one rule she followed strictly: not to mix business with pleasure.

The phone was ringing as she stepped out of the shower. Madison grabbed her oversized, terrycloth towel and reached the phone on the nightstand.

"Hello?" Madison said, sounding out of breath.

"Good morning, Madison."

Madison immediately recognized the voice as that of her best friend, Abigail. "What's up?" Madison asked. "You don't call me this early unless you are up to something. So what gives ?"

"Are you sitting down?" replied Abigail.

"No, I'm not sitting. I'm running a little behind this morning. Abigail, so tell me what you're up to," Madison said as she walked over to her closet to pick out today's outfit.

"I was just wondering if we could get together for dinner." Abigail paused, waiting for that to sink in, and then continued. "You know my boyfriend, Mark? He has this friend, and we want to set you up on a blind date." Abigail stopped, knowing full well that Madison was probably not even paying attention.

Madison paused at Abigail's idea. Yes, she had met Mark a few times and thought he was a great guy. Abigail was madly in love with him. "I appreciate you watching out for my love life, but I'm not interested. I have a full schedule this week and am on strict deadlines, which, by the way, I'm going to be late for if we don't hang up." Madison was beginning to feel edgy. She had important clients, and it was already 7:05 A.M. She had to be at her office by 8:30 A.M.

"Okay, Madison," Abigail replied. She knew to stop when she was ahead. "Maybe we can go to dinner in a couple of weeks."

"I'll let you know," Madison replied. "Now, I've got to go, Abigail. I'll call you later. Maybe we can squeeze in lunch one day this week."

Abigail sighed. "Okay, Madison. Have a great week, and don't worry, sweetie. You'll blow your clients away; you always do. Bye. Love you," Abigail said as she hung up the phone.

"Bye," Madison spoke into the phone, only hearing the dial tone.

Madison and Abigail met in college. They had various classes together but didn't really become friends until their sophomore year. They started sharing notes and comparing reports and realized that they had a lot in common. They had the same beliefs and knew that they were blessed to have found each other. They decided that they would rent an apartment together and split everything. It had worked out excellently.

They were both clean, liked to make good grades, and tried to excel in everything that they touched. They were both smart and beautiful and made an impact on everyone they met through their college years. No one on campus had anything mean or hateful to say about the best friends.

Madison and Abigail kept to themselves, studied, and pushed to make their futures bright. Madison went to interior design, and Abigail decided to go toward law and law enforcement. Now Madison owned her own interior design company, and Abigail was a top-rate criminal lawyer. Abigail was like Madison in a way; they weren't faithful in attending church every week, but they both knew that their faith was still present in their lives. They both had stressful jobs, but neither of them would have it any other way. They were a success, and they had each other to thank for that. They both pushed each other harder and harder to achieve their goals and aspirations.

Now, ten years later, they were just as close as ever. They still shared everything in their lives. Neither one of them had married yet. They were waiting for their true loves. Granted, they had both dated men, but what they wanted was more. They wanted a certain type of man; someone who had good morals, who would love them and work just as hard as they did. So far Madison had not found him, but Abigail thought maybe she had.

Abigail had met Mark about nine months ago, and she was deeply in love. Mark was the best boyfriend Abigail ever had. He was successful, and now Madison wondered if Mark did or would go to church. Madison had been so busy working that she hadn't had the church-faith talk with Abigail. She took down a mental note to have that talk with her as soon as she could. It was important to Madison that Abigail be with a good man and one that Abigail could depend on. Abigail was a bit high maintenance, and the pressures on her would make most men crazy. However, Mark treated Abigail like a queen. They complimented each other all the time and looked like they belonged together.

M adison looked at the phone feeling somewhat bad that she rushed Abigail, but she just didn't have time this morning. She glanced at the clock, now reading 7:30 A.M. She had to get with it this morning. Madison quickly went to her bathroom, blow dried her hair, stuck hot rollers in, and started applying her makeup. She then took the hot rollers out, brushed out her hair, and went to put on her tailored navy skirt and jacket. She had already picked this particular suit out when she was in the shower going over what was in her closet and what she felt like wearing today. Madison chose a pink satin shirt to go under the jacket. She felt like a power player.

Madison walked into the living room and kitchen, picking up paperwork, putting it into her briefcase, and started walking toward the door. She paused long enough to grab a banana and another cup of coffee from the kitchen island. She then walked out the door, locking the deadbolt behind her.

Glancing down at her amethyst watch, she discovered it was already 8:00 A.M. She had to hurry. Downtown Houston would be crazy at this time of morning. She opened her car door and put her briefcase and purse in the passenger seat and started up her Mercedes. She looked over at the passenger seat, and it dawned on her that no male had even been in that passenger seat. *Well,* she thought, *no one with any romantic intentions.*

She was rushing to get out of her neighborhood and got stuck behind an elderly man driving around twenty miles per hour. Madison bit her lip as she glanced at her clock. It read 8:07 A.M. She was working her way through downtown Houston and was speeding down Fifth Avenue when she saw the signal lights changing in front of her from green to red.

"Oh no, great" mumbled Madison as she hit the brake. She pulled up to the red light and sat there drumming her perfectly manicured fingernails on the steering wheel. She glanced down again to the clock and reached over and grabbed her cell phone to call the office. She hit the speed dial for the office and waited; it rang only once. Madison smiled at her efficient team.

"Good morning. Trent Design," answered the bright, cheerful receptionist named Sandi.

"Good morning, Sandi, it's Madison. Can I speak with Megan, please?" Madison asked, still watching the light.

"Right away, Miss Trent." Sandi sounded as though she were a little nervous for some reason.

"This is Megan," Megan Trent answered. Not only was she Madison's mom but also Madison's right hand employee. She used to be an accountant but retired and then took a few years off to relax and travel with friends. But she soon grew bored. Megan was relieved when Madison offered her something to do, and the pay wasn't bad either.

"Mom, I'm so glad that you're there already," Madison stated swiftly.

"Well, yes, Madison, it's 8:20 A.M., and I'm supposed to be here, and so are you. Speaking of, where are you?" Megan glanced over some last-minute paperwork while waiting for Madison's response. Her daughter was always on time, if not early, and if not, there was a reason.

"Mom, I'm stuck in traffic about three miles away from the office," Madison said, hurried. She didn't like her mother's motherly tone; it drove her nuts sometimes. "I just want you to go ahead and set everything up for our meeting this morning. Get all the copies ready, make sure the coffee is not too strong, and make sure that the pastries are fresh."

"I'll make sure everything is ready. I always do. Don't worry; everything will be great. You have prepared for this and are ready; your samples are excellent. Besides, the clients are not even here yet," Megan chirped.

"Okay, I'll see you as soon as I get there," Madison said nervously and disconnected the call. She threw her cell phone into her purse and mumbled under her breath, "This has to be the longest light ever." That's when she saw him. She looked closer and realized that the man in the truck next to her was absolutely gorgeous. She had never seen a man so, well, *hot*. He completely took her breath away; she had to swallow just to get her breath back. But she couldn't take her eyes away from him and continued to stare. There was something so mesmerizing about him. He had blondish-brown hair that appeared to be kept short and neat except for the little ponytail in back. His complexion was beautiful, not a blemish on it. "Oh no," she mumbled. She was caught looking at him and knew it. She tried to look away, but her eyes didn't want to leave what they found. He smiled, and his eyes lit up. Madison thought that she was going to pass out. It was getting hot in her SUV all of a sudden. Her pink blouse was starting to plaster against her skin as she tried to straighten it out. Thankfully, the light turned green and she exhaled. He nodded and started moving forward. Madison didn't know exactly know much time had passed, but it felt like that smile lasted all day. She watched as he started moving with the traffic. On the side of his truck, it read, "Mann Co." Her jaw dropped as she realized he was driving a wrecker.

Here I am, Madison thought, *driving a brand-new Mercedes and that beautiful man drives a wrecker? Am I getting desperate?* Before she could think about it anymore, the car behind her started to honk its horn.

"Wow," Zachary Mann thought out loud. He was just minding his own business, waiting on the light, and happened to glance over and see a beautiful woman staring at him. He was almost certain that he knew her type. *She is probably a major stuck-up snob,* Zachary thought to himself. *Just look at her in her high-dollar suit and her new Mercedes.* He had seen her throw her cell phone over to the passenger seat and chuckled to himself, thinking that she probably just had an argument with her boyfriend or husband, but he didn't think that he saw a wedding ring. "Oh well," mumbled Zachary. "There's a lot of fish out in the sea, and not all of them are snobs." Just then the light turned, and he started to cross into the intersection. Hearing a car horn, he looked back in his rearview mirror and saw that the stuck-up queen was still at the light. Zachary couldn't figure out what was wrong. He knew that it was nothing with her new car, so he just kept going.

Zachary was the owner of Mann Company, one of the leading repossession companies in the state, and was proud of what he did. It was long hours and hard work but well worth it. When he repossessed the vehicles, it was such an adrenaline rush, one that he enjoyed immensely. Mann Co. employed fifteen other people besides himself and had all seven trucks running at all hours of the night. He was always busy and did not have time for anything else, much less a relationship. He had dated a lot of different women, but none of them could understand his job and the hours that came with it. Needless to say, none of them lasted very long. That hottie in the Mercedes was something he would have liked to have, but he doubted that he could even get close to her, much less run around in her stuck-up, high maintenance circle.

* * *

"Okay, okay," Madison griped and glanced at her clock. It was only 8:23 A.M. Madison couldn't believe it; time felt like it was standing still. She started her SUV out and finally made her way to her two-story office with only three minutes to spare. Madison grabbed her briefcase and purse and headed for the door, which she smiled at. It was a beautiful, deep, cherry wood with the name Trent Design. As she entered the building, Sandi greeted her.

"Good morning, Miss Trent. Your clients just arrived and just sat down in the conference room. I believe that Megan is in there now getting them settled in for your presentation. I just know that it'll be great, Miss Trent."

"Thank you, Sandi." Madison rushed as she walked toward her office. As she unlocked her office door, she glanced around the spacious, colorful room. This is where she did her best work; this was her rest haven, her safe place. This was her ball field, and she had the home advantage. She quickly put down her purse and briefcase and got out her notes, proposal, and samples just as Megan walked in.

"Madison, it's about time that you arrived; your clients are waiting," Megan said matter-of-factly.

"Okay, Megan." Madison tried really hard not to call her mom at the office. As much as Megan did for Trent Design, she deserved the respect and the recognition. Megan worked extremely hard for Madison.

"Just give me one minute to freshen up and get my thoughts together," Madison added. Megan walked out of her office while Madison was putting on a fresh layer of burgundy lipstick. She felt herself getting flushed, and she had butterflies in her stomach. After all these years, she knew that her clients wouldn't make her feel like this. She paused and glanced in the mirror and was amazed to see herself smiling. Just the thought of that hunky mystery wrecker driver from this morning had left her feeling strange, almost warm and fuzzy. She chastised herself for getting so worked up. After all, he was just a wrecker driver.

"Madison, hurry up." Megan's voice grabbed her from her daydreaming.

"Okay, I'm right behind you." Madison sighed as she spritzed on a dab of her favorite perfume.

When Madison opened the door to the conference room, she glanced around and recognized two of the gentleman as Noah and Dylan. They were two of the bigwigs from the client's office. The few times that she had talked to either of them, they were quite funny. Madison knew that this meeting and contract were very important to her and her company. She had a reassuring feeling that this was a done deal. Still standing, Madison addressed the table.

"Good morning, ladies and gentlemen. I'm Madison Trent, and this is my assistant, Megan. Welcome to Trent Design. Let's get down to business, shall we? This morning, I have designed and prepared five samples that I am positive you will know is a perfect solution and design for all of your offices."

Madison paused long enough to make eye contact with each and every one of the eight people present. When she made eye contact with Noah, he smiled and winked. When she glanced at Dylan, he gave her a smile and a thumbs-up sign.

Madison continued smiling. "I have taken into account every need and desire that the eight of you have told me you have for your offices. Please feel free to ask questions and pass these samples around. Feel them, tug on them, whatever you want. I want this to be a comfortable and fun presentation. Please also help yourselves to the coffee, juices, and pastries." Megan was already passing around all the different samples and swatches of fabric.

Madison knew she had this in the bag, and oh boy, she thought, this was going to be a very big bag. The meeting continued for another two and a half hours. At 11:00 A.M., all of the eight clients had agreed on the blue, tan, and mauve samples. Madison was about to burst. Not only was her company redesigning over one hundred offices and lobbies, but her company name, Trent Design, would be proudly displayed in the lobbies on each and every floor that was decorated. Madison was sure this would gain her even more business. Trent Design was already busy. Before this new project was over, Madison would have to hire more employees. She was just about to bounce off the walls she was so happy. On the way out the door, Dylan and Noah stopped to congratulate her on such an outstanding presentation.

"Madison, you were positively radiant," stated Noah. "Your color schemes and layouts are incredible; they are exactly what we have been looking for. We have even shopped around for other designers, and I'll tell you that no one does it as good and as well presented as you do."

"Thank you, Noah. I was relieved to see a couple familiar faces this morning," Madison replied.

Dylan stepped toward Madison and placed his hand on her shoulder. "You did fabulous this morning. Let's go out and celebrate tonight. Would you care to go to dinner with me?" Dylan asked shyly. Madison tried to take a step back. Not only was she shocked, but she also realized that she was already against the wall. There was nowhere to go. She was flattered but had a solid vow never to mix business and pleasure.

"Noah, I'm really flattered, but I'm so far behind on getting ready for my upcoming interior design conference that I have to get caught up in the next couple of weeks. Please accept my apology," Madison replied as she placed her hand toward her heart. She was not lying, but she didn't want to go out with a client; it was a big no-no.

"Well, okay," Dylan said as he took something out of his suit coat and then reached for Madison's hand. "Maybe next time." As he was preparing to leave, Madison noticed that he had left his business card in her hand. She looked up, and Dylan winked at her as he walked down the hall. Madison turned to go back into the conference room to straighten and gather her contracts and samples. She looked back down at the business card and noticed that Dylan had written his home phone with the written message, "Call me." She shook her head, allowing her long hair to sway as she placed the business card on the table. She was too busy for a relationship. She thought, *Now, if it would have been that hunk that I saw this morning, it might be a different story.*

"Stop it, Madison," she said out loud to herself. It was crazy to think about a man she had only seen once; she didn't even know his name. She was still trying to concentrate and gather contracts and samples when Megan butted into her thoughts.

"Stop what, Madison?" Megan asked curiously.

"Oh, nothing," Madison said, startled. She didn't even hear Megan walk into the room.

"Oh, come on, sweetheart," Megan said, trying to put the mom act on. "You can tell me."

"Nothing. I was just thinking out loud," Madison replied as she tried to finish collecting all of the paperwork and swatches and started down the hall to her office. She noticed that Megan was right behind her. She hated when her mom could see through her excuses. Megan followed Madison into her office and shut the door behind them.

"Okay, Madison. What is going on? Is something wrong? Are you ill or not feeling well today?" Megan asked seriously.

"No, Mom. Nothing like that," Madison replied as she sat down in her chair at her desk. Megan sat in the chair in front of her, wanting to watch and observe her daughter's expressions. Madison looked like Megan, yes, but she had just a twist of her daddy's eyebrows and nose. Madison's dad had passed away five years ago, and Madison didn't talk about it at all. It was a really hard time for Madison; she always seemed to be a daddy's girl. Megan shook her head, more for herself then anything. She still missed her late husband so very much.

"Mom, why are you shaking your head at me?" Madison thought that her mom could see right through her. "Okay, I'll tell you, Mom." Madison leaned back in her chair and tossed all the waiting messages back on her desk.

"Dylan asked me to dinner," Madison explained. "I know what you're thinking. I should go to dinner with him. Well, it's not that simple. He's not even my type; I'm not attracted to him in any way, shape, or form."

Megan looked at her daughter and frowned. "Madison, you really need to go out and find you a mate. You're not getting any younger." Megan looked at her daughter and then continued, "Why not go out to dinner with Dylan? It's just dinner; he's not asking you to marry him or anything."

"Mom." Madison was losing her temper. "Dylan is a client, and you know how I feel about that. I never date my clients. That's a bad mix from the beginning. Besides, he's not my type. I already told you that." Madison exhaled as she was trying to get her temper under control.

"And just what is your type?" Megan inquired. "Do you even know what your type is?"

"Mom, I want someone who I can just look at and I have to catch my breath, someone who gives me butterflies when I hear his voice on the phone. Someone strong, beautiful, and masculine. Someone who is unwavering in knowing what he wants and going after it. Someone who will love me unconditionally and be loyal to our cause. But I also want someone who will argue with me and stand up for themselves. Someone with blue eyes, brown or blond hair, someone who is totally a hunk. Someone who believes the same as I do, someone who I can spend the rest of my life with. Someone who is just as passionate about his career as I am for mine but who will also know how to relax and have fun. I always remember the saying that Grandfather used to have—that if a guy really liked me, he would go to church with me. Well, all of this is the type of man that I'm looking for." Before she could even think about anything else, a picture of the mystery man flashed through her memory. He was so beautiful; she couldn't even think about it. She felt her cheeks flush. She was thinking about him, the wrecker driver. "Besides," Madison continued, "I'm only thirty-three. I still have plenty of time to get married and give you a grandchild, so don't worry," Madison stated matter-of-factly.

"Sweetheart, I'm not worried about the grandbaby. Granted, it would be nice, but I can wait. I just want you to have someone to do things with, a companion, someone who can look out for you. I just have one more question for you. When you were describing your ideal man, you acted as though you already had this man picked out. Do you?" Megan asked, then continued. "Besides, romance, candlelight, and the fairy-tale life are not real. It takes a lot of faith, patience, and communication to make a marriage successful. It is not easy; it takes work." Madison studied her mother and wondered why her mother never remarried.

"Didn't you have the perfect marriage to Daddy?"

Megan looked at Madison, amazed that she even brought up her father. "Madison, while your father and I were married, we had a great, wonderful, fulfilling marriage. But it took a lot of work, and even then, it was no fairy-tale." Megan knew that she should stop or she would probably start crying. "Besides"—Megan laughed, trying to lighten the mood—"you didn't answer my question from earlier. Do you have this certain person picked out already? You act as though you are hiding something, or should I say *someone*, from me." Megan looked toward Madison, who had a slight smile forming on her beautiful, rosebud-shaped lips.

"I'm not hiding anyone," Madison stated. "I was just running late this morning, and when I came upon a stoplight, I saw this man. Oh, this is crazy. I don't even know his name."

"Go on," Megan encouraged.

"Well, Mom, he was absolutely beautiful. He is without a doubt a *man*. He is gorgeous. He looked like he would be totally fun, but he seemed like he could have a serious side to him as well. I don't know why I think all that; I only saw him in his truck. But again, I don't even know his name; so no, there is no one that I'm hiding." Madison relaxed and sat back in her chair, looking at her mother, knowing that she was going to say something.

"Madison, you never know. Maybe you will run into him again. But just remember the Cinderella fairy-tale never happens." Megan stood, knowing that this would be the end of the discussion. "I'll see you later, sweetie." She turned and left the office.

Madison sat there for a minute just thinking. No, she did not believe in the fairy-tale life, but she did believe in romance, and she did have faith that she would find her Mr. Right. She thought back to her parents' marriage. They always seemed so in love and so happy. They attended church together every week and were married for over twenty years. Madison didn't really understand at the time what had happened to make her parents get a divorce. She only knew that the day that her dad moved out completely changed her life, and now he had died.

Madison tried to not think about her father's death much; it still bothered her deeply, and it had been a long five years. Madison had accomplished so much; she wished that her dad could have seen it all and been involved. Her dad would have been proud of his little girl. Madison sat up in her chair and straightened her posture; she knew that she couldn't sit there all day thinking about her dad and this mystery man.

Time to get to work, she thought. She picked up her messages and began shuffling through them. She noticed that one message was from the director of the interior design association where she was going to be teaching a conference next month. *At least the conference is here in Houston,* she thought. She had to start preparing for a big contract and needed to be as close to home as possible. Other messages were from potential clients, and she had one from Abigail. She would call Abigail back later. She would let Megan and the assistants field all of the other calls and set up appointments to meet with the lucky clients-to-be. Madison glanced down at her watch; it read 1:00 P.M. She couldn't figure out where the day flew to. At the same time, her stomach growled, and she realized she had missed lunch. She pondered just for a moment and then decided that she was going to take the rest of the day off. She never did that; everyone called her a workaholic, and it was probably true. But she didn't have anything else to do or anyone to occupy her time. She called her receptionist, Sandi, and told her that she was going to be working from home the rest of the day.

"Are you ill, Miss Trent?" asked Sandi, worriedly.

"No, Sandi. I just feel like taking a couple of hours off. Please field all of my calls. I'll see you tomorrow." Madison placed the phone back on the hook and then started straightening her desk up. Madison gathered up her briefcase and purse and headed for the door.

She couldn't remember the last time she took the afternoon off to work or to play, much less leaving the office when it was still daylight outside. She was going to make the most of her afternoon off. As she started up her SUV, she decided what she would do. First, she'd stop by the mall, then grocery store, and then home to a nice, long, bubble bath before settling down to start working. As she headed toward home, she mentally took notes of where all of her stops were. She parked her SUV in the mall parking lot and turned off the engine. Madison sat there and just soaked in her surroundings for a brief moment. "It's all about me," she kept telling herself. Madison was one of those people who, if she was not at work, felt guilty for playing hooky. Even though she was the boss and owner, it still made her feel bad. But today was all about her. Maybe she would buy a new business suit and shoes, maybe some makeup. Who knew? She just knew that she was going shopping.

She felt a bit giddy as she walked into the mall. She had been so busy for the last couple of months, that she hadn't had any time to do any shopping other than the occasional grocery store run. Plus, she couldn't get her mind off of the gorgeous hunk that she had met at the stoplight that morning. So hopefully shopping would distract her from daydreaming about the jaw-dropping mystery man all day. Besides, she was still a bit concerned that she was dreaming of just a wrecker driver. She wondered just what kind of man he was. Did he own a house, big or small? Did he have savings? Did he go to church? Did he party? Was he married? All these thoughts were running through her mind; she didn't know anything about this wrecker driver and wondered just what kind of man he could be. She was more high maintenance than that. She wanted more in life and didn't want to have someone riding on her coat tails. She sighed loudly and tried to forget the man that stopped her heart.

As Madison walked up and down the aisles of her favorite department store, nothing seemed to speak out to her. She wandered around, and found herself looking in the shoes and purses. She glanced down at her purse and thought it was a bit worn out and had seen better days. She then went around looking for a purse that spoke to her and found a rack that had a wide variety. She looked at the sizes; she never knew if she needed a small or large purse. She seemed to always get the big purses and then lose stuff in the bottom and had to dig around for it. She finally decided on two different purses. Then Madison walked around and found a pairs of shoes on sale. Today was her lucky day. "*Hmm*," Madison said to herself. Shopping was relaxing, but she was a long way off from putting the mystery man out of her mind, it was starting to irritate her. She couldn't get the butterflies to stop flying in her stomach. Madison smiled to herself as she thought about the mystery man again.

"Ma'am, could I help you with some of these?" the perky salesperson asked.

Madison jumped with a startled, "What?" She was upset that she was taken from daydreaming.

"Oh, I'm so sorry, just off in la-la land," Madison replied. Madison gathered the rest of her purchases and was ready to check out. She placed the items on the counter, and the perky salesperson came over to check Madison out.

"Did you find everything you were looking for?" the salesperson asked.

"Yes, I did. Thank you so much," Madison answered.

"Did you see these dresses that we have on sale? We have a cute sundress that would look great on you." She was trying hard, Madison noticed.

Madison looked over at them and realized that they were really pretty.

"No, I haven't seen them. Would you hang on for a minute? " Madison asked.

"Certainly. Take your time."

Madison walked over and started looking through the sundresses. She ended up buying the striped sundress that would match the pair of shoes. Now she had everything, and she smiled. She paid for her purchases and left the store. She was walking down the mall when she realized that she was headed for The Body Shop, which kept tons of different types of lotions and perfumes. It was probably a good fifteen minutes before she made up her mind and bought some lotion, bubble bath, and perfume. Now she was set for whatever came her way. She felt foolish for buying all of these items but realized that she didn't splurge much, mainly because she was too busy working. "Next stop, grocery store," she mumbled to herself.

As Madison walked into the grocery store, she made a mental list of things that she needed. She walked up and down each aisle, picking up something from every aisle. She had just picked up an orange when she looked up and saw a man standing with his back to her. Madison took a deep breath and thought, *This isn't happening.* The man had brown-blondish hair and a little ponytail hanging down. Madison thought that this was too good to be true. Just then the man turned around, and Madison noticed that the man wasn't her dream man. In fact, he was an older gentleman, still attractive, but not the man that she had seen this morning. Madison let out a sigh and finished up her grocery shopping. Just as she was putting her groceries in the back of her SUV, her cell phone rang.

"Great," Madison muttered, "so much for my afternoon to myself." Her cell phone continued to ring.

"Hello?" Madison said as she was getting in behind the wheel.

"Hello, Madison. This is Winston Bradford. I'm calling about the upcoming interior design conference." The voice sounded soothing and calm.

"Yes, sir. This is Madison Trent. I'm looking forward to the conference as well. Really excited about showing the ideas and samples." Madison was wondering how he got her cell phone number and why he didn't call the office and speak with Megan.

"Well, the reason that I'm calling is that I would like to fax over the itinerary of the conference and let you choose which seminars you would like to teach and which ones you want to attend. There is also a dinner on the last night; it is a black tie affair. Would you like to attend?" Mr. Bradford asked.

"That sounds wonderful. Please fax the itinerary to me, and I will look at it and get back to you in a couple of days. Would that be all right? As for the dinner, I would be honored to attend!" Madison said shyly.

Mr. Bradford replied, "Yes, a couple of days would be great. The sooner the better. I would like to let you know that you'll be seated at the honor table at the front of the conference. Could I book you a seat for an escort?"

Madison could feel herself blushing and responded, "It would be truly an honor. Yes, a second seat would be appreciated. I will be bringing my mother, who happens to be my assistant, to the dinner. May I also reserve a table for my staff at this dinner? I know that they will all be excited to attend."

"Yes, Miss Trent. I will get everything arranged and send the itinerary to you promptly. Good day," Mr. Bradford said smoothly and hung up.

Madison felt so giddy; she had been waiting for this conference for a while and was so excited that she was going to be at the honor table and be able to pick and choose what she taught and attended. Madison pulled into her driveway, excited about the upcoming conference, but still had a lot of deadlines to get finished before she could even think of getting ready for that.

Once she had her groceries put up, she placed her briefcase on the kitchen table and went to the cabinet to get herself a glass. She then went to the fridge for a bottle of wine. That would calm her nerves. She filled up her glass to the rim with wine and headed toward the bathroom to start her bubble bath. On her way, she remembered to grab the new bubble bath out of the sack as she started down the hall.

As she started her bubble bath, she realized how quiet it was in her house. She had not been home this early in a long time. The neighborhood was really quiet outside also; Madison loved it. She had added her new bubble bath to the water, and before long, the entire bathroom and bedroom smelled like a heavenly scent ready to take her up and away to where there were no deadlines and no messages to return and where there wasn't a hunky wrecker driver. The smell was divine. Madison wished that she could have this smell around her all the time, especially in her office, but then again she probably would not get any work finished.

She walked into the kitchen to refill her wine glass and decided that she had better take her cell phone into the bathroom with her just in case it rang. Then she would know who called, and then she could choose if she wanted to answer it or not.

Madison walked into her bedroom, checking on the tub to make sure that it didn't overflow. She had designed this bathtub; it was extra large and could hold a lot of water. Madison liked the water level high, so when she stepped into the tub, the water came almost to her shoulders. Madison slipped out of her suit jacket and skirt and laid them on the bed; then she took off her hose and threw them in the hamper. She carelessly put up her hair in a clip and stripped off the rest of her clothes and walked into the bathroom, grabbing her robe as she went. Madison's body was in shape. She had a lean torso and long, firm legs. Her stomach was taut. Overall, her body was very attractive. Madison knew that she had a nice body, but nothing that would make anyone jealous or anything, or so she thought.

Madison took her glass of wine and set it on the side of the tub. She then turned on the portable CD player that she had in the bathroom and played a classical CD. She turned on the jets and took the two steps up on the tub, putting one leg in, and then the other. She then sat down, letting the water merge with her body. She leaned back against the back of the tub and closed her eyes, letting the bubble bath soothe away her worries and stress. Her mind started working, and she willed herself to completely relax and to let her mind wander where it wanted. And it slowly shifted to the mystery man she saw today.

There he was, standing there looking at her with a sly smile on his beautifully shaped lips. Madison was walking toward him with an outstretched hand. Her mystery man said in a deep, sensual voice, "Hi, I'm …"

Suddenly, Madison opened her eyes; her cell phone had been ringing. She didn't know how long the phone had been ringing but thought that it must be someone calling back because it kept ringing and ringing. Madison blinked her eyes and tried to figure out what happened. The bubble bath was still hot, or at least Madison thought it was. She grabbed her phone from the counter and noticed that the number was her mother. She opened her cell phone and answered.

"Hello?"

"Madison, what are you doing? I've been trying to get a hold of you for the last fifteen minutes. I've called this phone at least three times. Are you sleeping?" Megan asked softly.

"Hi, Mom. No, I was just resting and must have dozed off. Sorry that I didn't get to the phone earlier," Madison replied. She still felt somewhat disorientated; she didn't remember the last time that she had awakened and felt tired.

"I just wanted to call and make sure that you're okay. You left the office so abruptly that I was worried. You must be extremely tired. I'll let you go, sweetie, and I'll talk to you in the morning." Megan stated.

"Okay, Mom. I'll talk to you later. Love you," Madison responded and folded up her cell phone. Madison leaned back in the tub again and wondered what would have made her mom call her on her cell phone. *Oh well*, she thought *I can deal with whatever tomorrow*. She turned her attention to the bubbles again and closed her eyes. This time she wondered what the name of the wrecker driver was; it was really driving her crazy. And to make things more interesting, he was only a wrecker driver.

"Hello?" Madison answered her phone. It was a beautiful Saturday morning, and she was enjoying it immensely. It was only 10:30 A.M., and Madison had already cleaned her house and had her laundry finished.

"Hey, Madison. What are you up to this morning?" Abigail asked.

"Oh, nothing really. I woke up early, so I already have all my chores finished. I should work on a client's proposal, but not quite that motivated yet, so I'm just hanging out. Why? What's up?" Madison replied.

"Well, Mark and I were planning to go out for dinner. We would like you to come. Mark's friend is going to be there, and he would really like to meet you." Abigail paused and then continued. "I know what you're thinking, Madison, and it's not like that. We aren't trying to set the two of you up. We're just getting together as friends. His friend knows this too. We are all just friends. He doesn't think it's a blind date, so you can relax. If you like each other, fine. If not, that's fine also."

"Oh, Abigail. I really appreciate what you're trying to do, really, but I just don't know. Do you even know anything about Mark's friend? Do you even know his name? What he looks like? What he does for a living?" Madison said and sighed.

Abigail took a deep breath. She knew that Madison would ask her a thousand questions; she always did. She was surprised that Madison didn't ask what the man's blood type was. But it did not matter; Abigail was prepared with all the answers.

"Well," Abigail started, "his name is Luke, and he works with Mark." Mark worked as a construction contractor for a major Dallas company that had an office in Houston. Mark and Luke worked together on a lot of jobs. They were currently working on a job on the outskirts of Houston in one of the finest housing communities around. Basically all that Mark did was supervise the job and make sure that only the finest materials were being used. Mark rarely ever got his hands dirty, but when he did, he enjoyed it. Luke was just like him; they had a lot in common. They both took pride in their jobs and did it in the highest regards. Luke was the head foreman and worked directly with Mark. Luke had gotten a divorce a little over a year ago and did not really want to date, but Mark had encouraged him to at least meet Madison. After all that Mark had told him about Madison, she sounded like she had her head on her shoulders and that she was worth meeting.

Abigail was still rattling. "Luke is thirty-five years old, has been married once, and does not have any children. He has green eyes and dark hair."

Madison halfway listened to the man that Abigail was describing. She knew that she would just have to go or Abigail would never let her hear the end of it.

"And he also has a nice body." *Boy,* Madison thought, *she really did her homework on this one.* Madison then tuned in again to Abigail.

"He is pretty tall, maybe about six feet or so. You know how I am with height, Madison. Luke is Mark's head foreman on most of Mark's jobs that he has. He is really successful, makes really good money, but like you need to worry about that. " Abigail took a breath and waited for Madison to respond.

Madison took a quick summary of what Abigail just told her—tall, dark, and successful.

Surely he can't be all that boring, Madison thought.

"Okay, Abigail," Madison replied. "I'll go tonight, but you, my very best friend in the world, must come over and help me plant flowers. Then," Madison continued before Abigail could interrupt, "we can get dressed together over at my house. We'll go and meet the men at the restaurant." Madison paused and let Abigail soak in her only option.

"Well," Abigail started, "I guess you win, as always. What time would you like me over there?" Abigail asked.

"Why don't you come over at 3:00 P.M.? That will give me a chance to run to the Flower Shack and buy my flowers. I think this year I'm going to buy a variety of flowers, not just one kind. What do you think?" Madison asked curiously.

"Well, Madison, whatever floats your boat. You know that I don't do much with flowers. I still don't understand why you don't hire someone to do your landscaping for you. You make enough money for it," Abigail said nervously. Abigail knew that Madison didn't like to show off all her success and money, well, not as much as Abigail, that is.

"Planting flowers is one of my few luxuries left. It's relaxing for me to get out in my yard and plant flowers and just be outside and not behind my desk all day. I like doing my own gardening, cooking, cleaning, and everything else. You know that I'm not quite as flamboyant as you are. I know that I have money, but I still enjoy the little things in my life." Madison lectured a little more sternly than she would have liked.

"Okay, okay, you win," Abigail said, defeated. "I'll be over at 3:00 p.m. to help you plant some flowers. But remember, after our flower project we are going to pamper ourselves to get ready for tonight, okay? Love you. Got to run."

"See you soon."

Abigail hung up, leaving Madison listening to a dial tone for the second time this week.

Madison hung up the phone and sat there for a couple of minutes, wondering what she had just gotten herself into. Thirty minutes later, Madison was starting up her SUV and backing out of the garage. As she was going down Maple Drive, she happened to see a wrecker a few vehicles in front of her. Madison felt her heart start to beat a little faster, and her palms started to get clammy. She wanted to catch up with the wrecker just to get a quick glance to see if it was her hunk. Madison accelerated and passed two vehicles in front of her. Madison finally got to where she could make out the wrecker a little better. She got about half a car length behind the wrecker and strained her neck to try to see who was in the seat. Just then the man in the wrecker slowed down, and the man looked at her.

"Oh my goodness," Madison said. The man in the wrecker was not her hunk at all. In fact, it was an older gentleman looking a little scary for Madison's taste. Madison took a deep breath and was thankful that she was at the stoplight ready to turn down Eighteenth Street. Madison turned left and then turned into the parking lot of the Flower Shack. She turned off her vehicle and sat there laughing at herself. She couldn't believe that she actually chased down a wrecker just to see if her mystery man was driving. How desperate was she? Madison decided that she was going to have fun tonight and try not to think about the handsome mystery man in the wrecker.

Madison got out of her SUV and went to buy her flowers. The flowers were beautiful for this time of year. She bought some rose bushes, tulips, lilies, and rose moss for ground coverage. As she drove home, she started thinking of what she should wear on the date. She wanted to look sexy, but not too sexy. She wanted to look friendly and inviting, but not too much. Some people just looked at Madison and thought that she was a snob, and she didn't want to appear that way, especially when this meant so much to Abigail. She was always trying to meddle in Madison's life, and sometimes Madison would let her. Madison knew that Abigail would go all out; she always did. Abigail always looked like she just stepped out of the magazines. Whether she was in court or a night out on the town, Abigail dressed to impress. That was one thing that

Madison loved about her. Madison thought back to all the times that they went out together; they were such great friends. Madison could not picture her life any other way than having Abigail right there beside her. Abigail was always there for her. No matter what was going on or how busy they were, they always stopped for each other.

Abigail arrived at Madison's house at 2:45 P.M. Madison had to take a double glance to make sure that it was really Abigail. Timeliness was not Abigail's strong suit. Madison watched as Abigail got out of her shiny new Mercedes convertible and noticed that Abigail was reaching in the back seat to get something. Madison walked down the sidewalk and noticed that Abigail had three different bags, along with a cosmetic bag.

"Abigail, what are you doing with all of this stuff?" Madison asked curiously.

"Well, one bag is shoes, one is accessories, and the other is outfits, and of course you know what is in a cosmetic bag. I didn't know what I was going to wear, and I figured that you didn't have a clue either, so I brought some things. I want to look good tonight for Mark. This is the first time that I have really met his friend, I mean, well, you know," Abigail stated.

Madison interrupted. "Are you saying that you have never met Mark's friend that you are trying to set me up with?"

"Well, if you would have let me finish, I have met him, but I've only met him at the job site. I've talked with him a couple of times. I let Mark be the one who is the matchmaker in this one." Abigail paused, knowing that Madison wasn't going to like hearing that.

"Okay, Abigail, but only as friends. Besides, I could probably use a night out," Madison stated. "Now, let's get this stuff inside, and then we're going to plant some flowers." She grabbed two of the bags and decided that Abigail could manage with the rest.

"Okay, I'm right behind you. I can't tell you how excited I am to be planting flowers on this beautiful day," Abigail said. Madison could hear the sarcasm in her voice. Abigail followed into the house behind Madison and headed straight to the guest room with her bags. Abigail had spent numerous nights with Madison and knew where everything was located.

Madison's house was beautiful, as well it should be, considering that she was an interior designer. Madison had three spacious bedrooms, two full baths, and a generous sized living room with an equally large den. She also had an office added in the back of her house. Madison loved her home. She had a massive deck built with planters. She enjoyed going into the backyard after a stressful day and inhaling the aroma of the flowers.

Madison had been home a few hours before Abigail arrived and had already taken the flowers into the backyard. She had also bought herself and Abigail each a pair of garden gloves; she did not want to ruin their immaculate manicures. Madison stopped in the kitchen while waiting for Abigail. She took out two glasses and filled them with lemonade. Abigail was just walking down the hall to the kitchen when Madison handed her the drink and gently pushed her outside.

"Madison, do we really have to plant all of these flowers? There are so many of them. What did you do, buy out the entire Flower Shack?" Abigail asked jokingly.

"No, I didn't buy a lot. I just bought enough to fill up all of my planters and hopefully have enough to fill some pots I have around here," Madison answered sweetly. "Here, I bought these for you." She handed the gloves to Abigail.

"Oh, thank you so much. I would hate to have dirt on my hands," Abigail said laughingly.

"I know. That's why I bought each of us a pair. I didn't want to hear you complain while you were trying to get the dirt out from beneath your fingernails before this big evening you have planned," Madison said with her own bit of sarcasm.

Over the next two and a half hours, Abigail and Madison planted the flowers and chatted about a million different topics, from the weather, to work, to sports, to fashion—you name it, they talked about it. When Abigail looked down at herself, she noticed that she was covered with dirt and was glad that she had on old clothes, some that she didn't care about. She glanced down at her watch and realized that it was already 5:30 P.M.

"Oh no. We've got to hurry and get ready. It's already five thirty, and I know that getting clean and beautiful will take us a while," Abigail said with a slight laugh.

"Okay, you go ahead and jump in the shower. I'll finish picking up the trash and will come inside in just a minute. Oh, and don't pick yourself anything to wear because I want first choice," Madison said, smiling sweetly.

"Oh, all right. Just hurry up. I don't want to be standing around with just a towel on all afternoon," Abigail stated as she got up and trotted into the house. Abigail was thrilled that she was going on a double date tonight. She loved Mark and could not wait for Madison to find a significant other so they could start to go out together all the time.

Abigail got into the shower and let the hot water just run down her lean body. She was not fat by any means. Yet when she compared her body to Madison's, she felt as though she got a little cheated. She was lean and strong but had more of an athlete's body and build. She was not as busty as Madison and had to really work at being fit, where it just seemed to happen to Madison, even though she didn't think so.

Abigail continued to let the hot water run down and soaked up the steam. She turned her thoughts to Mark and to how handsome he was. Mark had it all. She had been dating him for a long while now and thought he was the one. Mark was sweet and caring and always made Abigail feel like she was worth a million bucks. She had yet to have sex with Mark; she wanted to make sure that he was interested in her as a person and not just in a sexual way. They had kissed and cuddled, but she really wanted to wait.

She had made the mistake of losing her virginity in college, and man, did she ever regret that. The guy she was dating at the time told her all the right things, but once she gave in, he was a completely different person. Abigail had felt guilty for having given in and was trying to cope with her feelings all while the guy was completely uncaring. Finally after a few weeks, they broke up. Abigail had sworn off sex until she met the one, and by the one she meant the one she would marry. But trying to be a post-virgin in your thirties wasn't easy; every man you dated thought that you owed him something.

Abigail made a lot of first dates the last dates because she wouldn't invite them into her house for a nightcap. The men seem to think that the nightcap always was meant for them to stay the night, and she wasn't having any of that. No sex for her until she was married. She couldn't figure out why men couldn't understand that. What was wrong with them? Was dinner and a movie not enough anymore?

Then she met Mark. He was the first man she had met who didn't pressure her into making a decision that she wasn't 100 percent comfortable with. Abigail was a great catch, and she knew it, but people talked. Some men wouldn't even give her the time of day because they knew she wasn't going to put out, but Abigail didn't care. She was who she was. She knew that God had forgiven her for losing her virginity. She knew that she was saved by love and grace. She just didn't want to make the same mistake twice.

"Abigail, hurry up. I'd like to have some hot water too," Madison said, breaking Abigail's memories of her past.

"Okay, I'm finished," Abigail said as she turned off the water and stepped out into a terry cloth towel.

"Are you okay?" Madison asked cautiously. "You look kind of flushed. Do you feel all right?" Madison continued.

"Yes, I feel great. Nothing's wrong. I guess that I was just daydreaming," replied Abigail.

"Well, I'm going to jump in the shower now, but don't pick anything to wear until I get a chance to look at it all. I get first dibs," Madison stated as she stripped out of her flower-planting clothes and into the stream of water.

Abigail blew her hair dry and plugged in her curling iron. She wanted to look spectacular tonight. She could hear Madison humming but could not make out what the song was. She moved close to the shower door and could not believe her ears. Madison was humming some love song. Abigail wondered if something was going on that she did not know about.

"What are you humming, Madison?" "Oh, I don't know. I didn't even know that I was humming," Madison replied.

Madison was washing her hair and was surprised to hear Abigail question her about her humming. She really didn't know where that song came from. She wasn't thinking of much, other than she wished that she had a date with the wrecker driver that she saw yesterday. She quietly got onto herself for still thinking about him. She didn't know anything about him. She had to quit. She was going to make the best of this evening; she made the promise to herself. She stepped out of the shower to see Abigail looking through her closet. Madison didn't know what Abigail as looking for but thought that she would know soon enough.

"Madison, don't you have anything daring in your closet? I want to wear something that Mark will find amazing on me," Abigail said in her best sexy drawl.

"I don't know what I have in my closet, but you can't be looking oh so sexy and leave me looking normal. I don't even know this guy, and I don't want to look like a tramp the first time that I meet him. On the other hand, I don't want to look like a stuck-up princess compared to what you will be wearing," Madison said.

"Oh, you'll look beautiful in whatever you choose. I've laid out all of the outfits that I brought over. I'll give you first choice," Abigail said and pointed over to the bed. "Oh, Madison, did you happen to shave your legs while you were in the shower?"

"What kind of question is that? Of course I shaved my legs, but why would it matter if I did or not?" Madison asked questionably.

"Well," Abigail began, "you never know who you will meet or what will happen. I was just checking to see if you still think about things like that."

Madison looked at Abigail and asked her the same question. "Did you shave your legs?" Then Madison thought to ask other questions since Abigail had opened up the floor. "Have you had sex with Mark? I thought you wanted to wait?"

Abigail sat down on the floor and studied Madison for a moment before responding.

"No, Mark and I haven't had sex. You know how I feel about that. I do want to wait, but it is getting harder and harder to stay in control. I have talked to Mark about it, and he completely understands, but I can tell that he is getting frustrated as well, and to be honest, I'm a little worried that he may quit waiting for me. We have been dating for nine months, and these days probably all couples would have had sex, but I just don't feel right about it. I want to be married, and I want to know that the next time that I do have sex that I'm making love to my husband and that I will be spending the rest of my life with him."

Abigail paused, then breaking the awkward silence, she changed the subject. "Oh, Madison. We have to hurry. It's six forty-five, and I told the guys that we would meet them at eight. We don't have much time left, so hurry up and pick what you want to wear."

"I really don't know which one I should wear. What do you think?" Madison asked.

"I think that you should wear this." Abigail picked up a summer dress that was sleeveless and short. The dress was all navy with little white dots on it. It reminded Madison of the dress that Julia Roberts wore in *Pretty Woman,* only Julia's was brown and long.

"That's cute. What shoes do you have to go with it?" Madison asked Abigail as she held the dress up to her and looked at herself in the mirror.

"Here are the shoes; they match perfectly. I got these out of your own closet. I haven't seen you wear these. When did you get them?" Abigail asked as she handed the shoes to Madison.

"Oh, I've had those shoes for a while. I just never really thought that I had the appropriate outfit to wear with them, but this dress will work out just right." Madison paused. "What are you going to wear? I think that you should wear the red dress; you always look good in red with your skin tone. Wear that dress with these shoes," Madison said while digging in her closet for the shoes that she was looking for. "Here are the shoes. Do you like?" Madison asked. Abigail could not believe her eyes; the shoes were a shiny red with about a four-inch heel.

"Where did you get those? I love them, but I don't really think that they're your type." Abigail paused, waiting for a reaction from Madison.

Madison began to explain. "I bought them a couple of years ago for a Halloween party at the office. I wanted something totally out of character for me. It worked," Madison answered.

"Yeah, I would say so," Abigail said as she slid her foot into one of the shoes, thinking how lucky they were that they wore the same size.

⁕ ⁕ ⁕

Thirty minutes later, both Abigail and Madison were putting on the finishing touches to their outfits. They both wore little solitaires in their ears, a present that they had bought together when they graduated college.

"Ready, Abigail?" Madison asked.

"Yep, I'm ready. I have to say that we look gorgeous tonight. We're sure to make all the men's heads turn," Abigail said with a gleam in her eyes.

As they drove to the Pelican Bar to meet the guys, they were both in their own la-la lands. Abigail was thinking about Mark and how and when she was going to really have the relationship talk with him. She knew they were dating only each other, but she wanted to know where he thought they were headed. Although Abigail was an attorney, she still liked to enjoy her life and was ready for marriage and to maybe take a little risk. She wanted to have kids before she got any older. The whole marriage and kids idea had been on her mind a lot lately.

Abigail had had a stressful week in court. She was defending a man who was being accused of committing grand larceny. Abigail didn't know for sure if her client was guilty or not, but it was her job to keep him out of jail. She was a litigator, and a brilliant one. She had different law offices calling almost every week trying to get her to come and join their firm, but Abigail was happy where she was and intended to stay at Brown and Paul. She was hoping that they were going to ask her to become partner in the next couple of weeks. They were looking for someone, and everyone thought that Abigail was the best candidate.

Abigail was the best attorney around. If they didn't make her a partner, then Abigail was thinking about going out on her own and opening up her own practice. She hadn't told Madison yet; she wanted to know for sure what the future held for her. She didn't want to make any decisions quickly.

But tonight, she thought, *I'm going to kick back and enjoy my evening with the man of my dreams and my best friend.* Abigail had everything that she could ever want—a thriving career and more money than she knew what to do with. Abigail spent a lot of money, but she also invested it and saved a lot as well. Abigail didn't have any family close by, so she really didn't have much to spend it on. She had Madison, of course, but Madison had enough of her own money. Mark had his own money as well. One thing was certain; she wasn't going to marry or date someone who didn't have his own money.

She didn't want to have to take care of a man. She wanted someone with whom she could become a partner and work together to achieve their goals. She wasn't in the mood to support someone or to bail someone out of debt. She had paid her debts, and that was enough.

Abigail was ready to get married. She was ready to have children and the white picket fence around her home. She and Mark hadn't talked about anything so serious yet, but Abigail hoped that it would be coming

48

up soon. She was ready to tell Mark that she loved him and wanted to spend the rest of her life with him. But she was old-fashioned and wanted Mark to do the proposing down on one knee. Abigail giggled at the possibilities.

They arrived at the restaurant with only ten minutes to spare. Abigail and Madison looked around and didn't see Mark or Luke anywhere, so they went ahead and asked to be seated. The waiter took them to their table. Madison sat in the chair that could see the entrance. She wanted to be able to see this Luke guy before he could see her. She really didn't know what she was getting herself into. The restaurant was getting crowded. Madison scanned the room and was vaguely familiar with some of the faces in the restaurant. The Pelican Bar was a somewhat expensive restaurant, and not everyone could afford to dine and drink here. She recognized a couple of the people as clients. She hoped that no one would say anything to her, and she hoped that they would leave before she ate. She wanted to relax and enjoy herself and not have to think about what people thought about her. Abigail had taken out her compact and was checking her makeup to make sure that everything was in place. Madison was observing people and slowly drinking her tea when she saw Mark walk in. She quickly looked to the man beside him and almost choked on her drink.

"Are you all right, Madison? What's wrong?" Abigail asked.

"I'm fine, but look," Madison said while pointing. "Look at this Luke guy; he's very handsome. It caught me off guard. Usually the people you set me up with are just so-so, but you did good on this one, Abigail,"

Madison said while drying off her lips and smoothing down her hair.

"Oh, Madison, be quiet. Here they come," Abigail warned.

"Hello, sweetheart," Abigail cooed.

"Hello, Abigail," Mark said as he leaned down and gave her a kiss. "Hello, Madison. This is Luke Davidson. Luke, this is Madison Trent, and of course you know Abigail," Mark stated.

Luke extended his hand, and Madison shook his hand, but Luke also raised her hand to his lips and kissed it.

"It's a pleasure to finally meet you, Madison. Mark has told me a lot about you," Luke said sweetly.

"Hello, Luke. I'm glad to meet you as well. I anticipate that we will all have a great evening," Madison answered. "Hello, Mark. Always good to see you," Madison finished.

Both of the men sat down, and the waiter was right there to get their drinks, almost a little too fast, Madison thought, but he was trying to earn a living. Plus, the waiter could probably see money when it walked in the door. All four of them were dressed to the tee. Madison noticed the muscles underneath the material of Luke's solid, button down shirt. He looked really good but not like the man that she saw yesterday. *Stop it,* she told herself.

The four of them were looking over the menu when Luke and Madison started talking at the same time. "I'm sorry, Madison. Go ahead," Luke encouraged.

"Oh no. You go ahead. I was just going to ask what everyone was having for dinner," Madison responded.

"Well," Abigail butted in, "I'm going to have the

red snapper with potatoes and veggies. And I think that I'll have a salad as well." Abigail paused. "I'm hungry, and I really didn't eat anything while I was at Madison's planting flowers but a glass of lemonade and a couple of cookies," Abigail finished.

Madison started to object, but Mark broke in.

"Oh, Abigail, I was going to ask you how planting flowers went. Did you enjoy yourself?" Mark asked.

"Well, besides it being sweaty, dirty, and hot, I enjoyed myself. I enjoyed spending time with Madison, but I didn't understand why we had to plant flowers. I told Madison to hire someone to come and plant her flowers for her, but she always refuses," Abigail complained.

"Well, I think that I can answer that," Luke said. "If you don't mind, Madison?" "By all means," Madison challenged.

Luke paused, smiled at Madison, and then gave his attention to Abigail.

"She likes to plant her own flowers because it gives her a sense of originality and personality. She enjoys being able to pick and choose what flower and where to plant that one flower. It makes her feel free and relaxed." Luke paused and then continued, "Well, that's the way it makes me feel. So how did I do, Madison?" Luke asked.

Madison looked at Abigail and then Luke. "You answered perfectly. I do enjoy my time out in my garden," Madison responded.

Abigail sighed and then turned her attention back to Mark.

"So, honey, what are you going to eat tonight?" Abigail asked.

The waiter suddenly appeared and took their order. The conversation was really good; not too serious, but not silly. Madison found that she was really enjoying talking with Luke. Abigail and Mark were involved in somewhat of their own conversation.

"Honey," Abigail whispered, "why don't we take our drinks outside on the patio for a few minutes and give Luke and Madison some time to themselves? Besides, some clients just walked in, and I would love for you to meet them." Abigail paused and turned to Madison. "Excuse me, Madison. I just saw some clients come in and want to introduce them to Mark. Would you both please excuse us?" she asked.

Luke cleared his throat and said, "Sure, go on. I think that Madison and I can wing it until the two of you get back." "Okay, we'll be right back. If the waiter comes by, please order us another drink for dinner," Mark replied and got up and headed after Abigail.

Madison thought that something was going on with Abigail and Mark. She knew that they were leaving Luke and her by themselves so that it would force them to talk and get along. Madison really didn't mind; she enjoyed talking to Luke. *He is very intelligent and easy on the eyes,* Madison thought.

After Mark and Abigail said hi to her clients, they took a walk outside. The weather was still nice, and the restaurant had the patio decorated with plants of every color and candles all around—really a perfect setting. *A perfect setting for a proposal,* Abigail thought and then shook the thought out of her mind. Out of the blue,

Mark grabbed her hand, pulled her into a hug, and gave her an earth-shattering kiss.

"Thank you for our date tonight," Mark started. "You look beautiful. I guess this is a good place to tell you that I love you, Abigail. "

Abigail looked up in shock and amazement.

"I love you too, Mark. I really do," she said as she leaned up and gave him a kiss. After some time, Abigail said, "We had better head back. They are probably wondering about us." Mark squeezed Abigail's hand, and they both headed toward the table.

"Let me handle this," Mark said.

"Well, where have the two of you been?" Luke asked.

"We said hi to a client of Abigail's. You know how much they can talk. Then we walked outside for a moment," Mark answered as he pulled Abigail's chair out for her. Abigail winked at him and sat down. Abigail couldn't believe what had just happened. It was absolutely, positively the best evening of their relationship yet—the very first time they'd used the words "I love you." Now she would just have to have *the talk,* the talk about church and faith, to see where exactly Mark stood. She thought she knew, but she just wanted to make sure. They had talked briefly about church before. Now it was time to become serious and start attending together as a couple to prepare for a life together, if this is who God placed in Abigail's life.

Madison thought that Abigail looked different. It seemed like she had a slight glow to her face, but Madison just assumed that it was the wine.

Luke really liked what he knew of Madison. She was beautiful, intelligent, and gorgeous. He was glad that Abigail and Mark left for a few minutes. It gave him time to talk to Madison privately and decide if he liked her; and he did.

The night continued pleasantly for the group as they ate, laughed, and enjoyed light conversation. Madison was mid-bite when she looked up to say something to Luke; but her words wouldn't come out. Her eyes went toward the door, and she felt a gasp come from deep within her. The man, the mystery wrecker driver, was talking with the waiter. He was with a couple of other guys. No women were with them, for which Madison found herself thankful. "Madison, are you all right?" Abigail asked.

"Yes, I'm fine. My food just went down the wrong tube," Madison tried to say, her eyes never leaving the man at the entrance. Just then he laughed and looked around, and his eyes met hers. He nodded slightly, and then the waiter took him and his friends to their table. Madison didn't know what had just transpired, but he was the sexiest and most incredible man that she had ever seen. She calmly tried to continue eating as though nothing had taken place. She tried not to think that the man of her dreams was here in this restaurant; the same restaurant as her. She smiled and made herself get back into the conversation of her company. It took all the willpower she had to gracefully have a good evening, but she made it through the night and actually had fun.

* * *

Zachary Mann had been coming to eat at the Pelican Bar for years now; it was one of his favorites. He'd become such a regular that he was on a first-name basis with most of the staff. As he laughed at something the greeter said, something pulled his attention to the side. He took a double look and a deep breath; there she was, actually there—the woman from the stoplight. He nodded at her and smiled. Wow, she was beautiful. It seemed as though she was as shocked to see him as he was to see her. She looked sexy, from what he could see. He wondered who those people were with her. One man and the other woman looked all lovey-dovey and were obviously a couple, but who was the other man? As the waiter moved Zachary and his buddies to their usual table, Zachary was glad for once that they were in the back. Now he didn't have to be miserable all night looking at his goddess of beauty talking with some other man, probably her boyfriend or husband.

Zachary Mann woke up on Sunday morning with a headache and something that felt like a heartache. He didn't dare say anything to his mystery woman last night. It was weird. He had seen her two times in the last two days. Was it a coincidence? Zachary rolled over and looked at his alarm clock; it was 8:30. He had slept later than usual. He was surprised to find his bulldog, Spanky, snoring soundly beside him. Usually Spanky was up and ready to go outside, but not this morning. Zachary climbed out of bed and walked down the hall, yelling for Spanky to come on. After he let Spanky outside, he walked through his home. He had bought this older home about seven years ago. He loved it, although it needed a bit of remodeling.

On Sunday mornings, Zachary sometimes attended church. His parents attended church every Sunday, and they expected Zachary to be there as well. He enjoyed going. It gave him a fresh start to the week, and he knew that he needed all of the help and blessings that he could get. Zachary went into the bathroom and took a quick shower. It didn't take him long, and he was ready to walk out the door. Zachary couldn't get over the fact that he had seen his mystery woman two times already. He wondered if she would be at his church as well. Zachary told himself to get over it. He had better things to do today.

Zachary decided that he would skip church this week. It was early, and a lot of people slept in on Sundays, and maybe, just maybe, he could get a couple of vehicles picked up. Right before he left his office last night, about ten new accounts were faxed to him, and he wanted to work a couple and see if he could get a vehicle or two picked up. He enjoyed working even though his mother told him to let his employee's work—that's what they were paid for. When his parents weren't telling him how to run his business, they were after him to get married and have a couple of grandbabies. They were ready to be grandparents. Zachary actually thought about it and wouldn't mind having a couple of kids, but that meant he had to be married first. That was the hard part. He wasn't even dating anyone. His buddies tried to set him up all the time, but he was picky. The woman he was going to date had to be smart and mature. *Usually the women I date are dumber than a box of rocks,* he thought as he walked out the front door and locked it behind him.

As he drove to the office, he was thinking back to how beautiful the woman at the stoplight and at the restaurant was. It was so crazy that he had seen her multiple times now and didn't know anything about her. He really didn't know what was going on inside his mind, but he had to get it cleared. He had work to do and didn't have time to be thinking of a woman. Once at the office, he picked up the mail and noticed an announcement for an interior design conference coming up in little over a week. Zachary looked at the announcement and thought that he should maybe go to it. After all, he did want to get his home refinished. He wondered how he got this invite then remembered that a couple of months ago, his cousin, Ann, had dragged him to a home and garden show and had dropped his name in a drawing. Ann was always after him to register for drawings even though he never won. Silly, he thought, that maybe one day he would win something.

He knew for sure that his family wanted him to win with a wife and grandkids. He would be happy just winning a gift card or something, even though the idea of marriage did appeal to him, in a way. He wasn't getting any younger and thought he was ready to settle down. He just didn't know if a woman could handle his career. He was called at all hours of the night and sometimes had to work late. Could a woman handle this? He suddenly wondered if this woman he had seen for the last couple of days could handle his lifestyle. Laughing to himself, he knew he was losing his mind.

He scanned the itinerary and saw that one of the speakers was a Madison Trent. *Who is that?* he thought to himself. *Probably some old woman,* he thought. Zachary would call Ann and see if she could attend with him. He hated to go to functions like that alone. He continued to read the brochure and noticed that there was a black tie dinner on Friday night. He had never been to an interior design conference before but thought it was a little odd that they would be having a black tie evening. What kind of evening was he in for? But he was curious and decided that he would go to that as well. He enjoyed getting all dressed up and ready for a good time.

* * *

Madison woke up on Sunday morning with a headache as well. Once she had seen him, she just hadn't been able to concentrate the rest of the evening and had a very sleepless night. But she didn't want to leave the restaurant. She wanted to stay and watch and observe him. Unfortunately where Abigail had them seated, she couldn't see him. The mystery man had sat in the back, on the other side of the restaurant with his friends. Madison spent the rest of the night talking and hanging out with Luke, who was really nice. Luke wanted to take the evening home, but Madison sweetly backed out of it. She got out of bed and walked into the kitchen, reaching for the aspirin and a cup of coffee. Madison had to start going over the upcoming design conference; she had less than two weeks to get her material prepared. As she walked over to her briefcase, she paused and reminisced on her date last night. She really did enjoy Luke's company. He was sweet and friendly and very hot. She opened up her briefcase and started taking out the paperwork. She had to review contracts and get the samples ready. She also had to decide what exactly she was going to teach on and get all of that prepared. As she sat down at the table, ready to go over her paperwork, the phone rang.

"Hello?" Madison answered.

"Madison, hi. It's Luke." He sounded so nice.

"Hi, Luke. I was hoping you would call. I had a lot of fun last night."

"Good. I'm relieved that you had fun. I wondered, since you had such a great time, if we could get together later on today and get a bite to eat or something." Luke paused. "It's a beautiful day, and I was thinking we could go out on my boat and maybe have some lunch." Luke really hoped that Madison agreed to come with him. It would be the first time he'd had a woman on his boat.

"Well, I have to go over some paperwork today, but I think that I can squeeze in a little play time. Let's see. It is 10:45 right now. What do you say to noon? That way I can get ready and start some paperwork. What would you like me to bring?" Madison asked and started giving Luke directions to her home. She found that she was smiling.

Luke smiled and replied, "I think that I know right where your house is. I have done some work over in that area. Actually, you don't need to bring anything. I'll have the boat stocked and loaded with all kinds of food. Do you like ham, turkey, and things like that?" Luke asked.

"Yes, I like all of that. Are you sure that I can't bring anything?" Madison questioned.

"If you really want to bring something, bring a dessert. Whatever you like is fine with me, I'm not picky. But don't worry about sunscreen or towels. I have plenty on the boat. I'll pick you up at noon. Get ready—this is going to be a day you won't forget. Bye." Luke hung up.

Madison hung up the phone and sat there wondering what she had gotten herself into. She thought that Luke was attractive and really nice, but to be on a boat with only a swimsuit on was a different story. *Oh well*, she thought, *might as well go out and enjoy this.* Besides, the man that she really wanted didn't even know her.

Madison walked over to her dresser and opened it up to try to find a swimsuit. She hadn't gone swimming in about a year. She wasn't even sure if she had a decent swimsuit. After digging through her drawer, she discovered that she only had a two-piece, which she just wasn't comfortable wearing in front of a guy she'd just met. Starting to panic, she picked up the phone and dialed Abigail. Abigail always went to the lake. Surely she would have a one-piece that Madison could borrow.

"Hello?" Abigail answered.

"Hey, Abigail! What you doing?" Madison tried to sound as normal as possible.

"Oh, nothing really, just sitting around trying to decide what Mark and I are going to do today. Why? What's up?"

"Well, don't get excited and don't read anything into this, but Luke called and has invited me to go boating with him this afternoon. I was looking, and I only have a two-piece, and I really want to wear a one-piece. So I thought that I would call and see if you could bring a one-piece over to me." Madison paused, knowing that Abigail was getting happy and that she always made something out of things like this.

"Oh, Madison, I'm happy for you. I think that you'll have a great time. I don't know why you don't want to wear a two-piece; you have the body for it. But I don't want to get into that right now with you. I will look in my drawer, and I'll bring over what I have," Abigail said.

"Okay, see you in a minute," Madison stated and hung up the phone. She went into the kitchen and decided that she would make brownies. Glancing at the clock, she saw she had forty-five minutes before Luke was supposed to be there. *I have time,* she thought. She made the brownies and placed the pan in the oven. Madison then walked into the bedroom, dug into the closet and finally found a beach bag and a pair of sandals. She packed a towel, sunscreen, sunglasses, and a book in her bag and placed it on the sofa with her purse. Although Luke said he had towels and sunscreen, she just felt more comfortable taking her own stuff. Besides, the towel he could offer her might not even cover her up. She giggled thinking she was being a bit dramatic, but she would rather be safe than sorry.

Ten minutes later, Abigail showed up with a handful of swimsuits. Madison was getting somewhat nervous, why she really didn't know.

"Hi, Madison. I brought over all that I could find," Abigail said as she walked in the house. She went toward the bedroom and threw all of the suits on the bed.

"Thank you. I really appreciate you bringing these over here. I was getting nervous and didn't know what I would wear," Madison said as she began to pick up the suits and look them over.

"These suits are really cute. I want one that covers me, but I don't want to look like I'm wearing a turtleneck," Madison finished.

As the two women looked over the swimsuits, Madison glanced over at the clock, and it was almost noon. Madison had to get everything together. Right at that time, the oven started ringing, signaling that the brownies were finished. Madison went to the oven and set out the brownies to cool and then went back into the bedroom to pick out her suit.

She quickly tried on a blue suit and walked out for Abigail to comment on.

"Wow, that suit looks awesome on you. I think that it looks better on you than it does on me," Abigail stated and winked at Madison, she then continued, "I think that you're going to have a great time. I want all of the details when you get home."

Just at that time, the doorbell rang. Abigail excused herself to go and answer the door while Madison finished getting her clothes ready and herself ready too. Abigail could tell that Madison was a bit nervous, but this was going to do her some good, Abigail thought as she walked to the door.

"Hey, Luke. Madison will be right out. She's just getting her things ready. Why don't you come on in?"

"Wow, this is a nice house. Did Madison do all the decorating herself?" Luke asked as he sat down on the sofa. "Why don't you ask me yourself?" Madison said with a slight laugh as she walked into the living room.

Luke stood and reached over to give Madison a quick peck on the cheek.

"All right, I will. Did you do all the decorating yourself? And by the way, you look great. Are you ready to go?"

"Yes, I did all the decorating, and yes, I think that I'm ready to go. Just let me grab my bag, and I made some brownies," Madison said as she walked over to the kitchen.

"Abigail, will you lock up when you leave?" Madison asked and smiled at Abigail.

"Sure, you guys go ahead and go. Have a good time," Abigail said.

"We will," Luke stated as they headed out the front door. They reached Luke's SUV and started on their way.

"Where is your boat at?" Madison asked.

"I leave it at the marina. I really don't want to have to hook it up and drag it every time I go to the lake. I don't go as much as I should, but I'm really looking forward to this afternoon," Luke commented. Madison settled in the seat and felt very comfortable with Luke. She wasn't sure why, but was happy that her nerves were settling down and planned on having a fun day.

Thirty-five minutes later, they pulled into the marina. They both got out of the SUV and gathered up their bags and towels. Luke led them down the marina to the boat named *Lighting Bolt*. Luke held out his hand as he mentioned what boat he was going to. Madison's jaw about fell open. This boat, *Lighting Bolt*, was huge. It had to be at least forty-five feet long. It was a cabin cruiser, and it was beautiful. Madison was in awe. They got aboard, and Luke gave her the grand tour as they put the brownies on the counter. It was magnificent. Soon after the tour, Luke started the boat, and they pulled out of the marina.

"You can change clothes down below if you want to go ahead and put on your suit and catch some sun. You can put your belongings on the bed or wherever you would like. Make yourself at home," Luke said.

"Thank you. I'll go below for a moment and put my stuff up and change. I really appreciate you asking me to come out today. I'm looking forward to having a good time and getting some relaxation," Madison said and then headed down below. When Madison got below, she looked around a little more than she had when Luke was giving her the tour. She took in the colors and the designs as well as the plush carpet that she walked on. She checked out the bathroom and took her bag in with her. She quickly stepped out of her shorts and tank top to reveal the swimsuit that she had worn. She had to admit that she looked good. She quickly did a checkup on her hair and swimsuit. She folded up her clothes and placed them in her bag, got out her towel and sunscreen, and grabbed her book. Who knew? Maybe she could read a bit, but she seriously doubted it. She walked out of the bathroom and placed her bag on the bed. There, she took a deep breath, grabbed her towel, and headed up to top deck.

As she took that final step up to the deck, Luke's eyes met hers.

"Wow, you look gorgeous," Luke said, and he meant it. He knew that Madison had a great body, but he had no idea that it looked like this.

Madison had to suck in a breath to make sure that she was not dreaming. In front of her stood Luke, and he looked pretty amazing himself. While she had been down below, he had changed into his shorts, and now he stood before her with no shirt on. She wasn't prepared for how attractive he'd be without his shirt on. She could tell that he had been to the gym, probably every day, as his chest was perfectly muscular. His stomach had amazing abs, and she was now drooling on herself. She felt herself getting hot and thought it must be the weather.

"Thank you. You look pretty good yourself," Madison replied, trying not to blush. She was a little embarrassed. She hadn't experienced anything like this in such a long time. She hadn't had the man-woman feeling in a while. Madison smiled and noticed that she felt a little nervous even though she thought she was just friends with Luke. After all, they had just met last night.

Over the next four hours, Madison and Luke talked about everything in their lives. Madison felt at ease talking with Luke, and they didn't have to force the conversation to happen. While they ate, Luke brushed up against her, and Madison felt a slight butterfly sensation in her belly; not an ambush of butterflies, but maybe just a couple. When Luke handed her a glass of lemonade, he leaned over and placed a kiss on her lips. Madison stood there letting this gesture soak in. Luke had just kissed her. She wasn't sure what she should do. His lips were warm and soft and seemed so full of need. Luke's voice interrupted her thoughts.

"I hope that I didn't step over my boundaries. It was just that you look so beautiful, and I have wanted to do that since you stepped on the boat," Luke said.

"Oh, no. It was nice. It's just that I wasn't expecting that," Madison replied. She took a deep breath and leaned over and kissed Luke back. Luke's hand reached around Madison's back and held her close. Madison felt herself tighten and wasn't sure what she should do. It wasn't every day that some gorgeous man kissed her. Luke kissed her again, and Madison felt the butterflies again. She wanted to like Luke. He seemed like such a good guy, maybe a little bit too good, but in the back of her mind was her mystery wrecker driver. Now, if she could kiss him … Her imagination took off. Her mind registered who and what she was thinking about, and she stepped back from Luke abruptly.

"Luke, I'm sorry," Madison said as she looked flushed, and her cheeks were burning. Madison couldn't believe what had just happened. She had been kissing Luke, this really nice man, while she was thinking and daydreaming about the man she saw last night. She knew that this wasn't fair to Luke.

"No need to apologize, Madison. I enjoyed it, and you seemed like you did too. Why did you pull away?" Luke asked.

"I don't know," Madison replied. "I guess that I wasn't used to this idea. You know, of this." Madison moved her hands back and forth between the two of them. "I'm old-fashioned, and all of this is moving a bit too fast for me to grasp in one day."

"I'm sorry if I came on a little strong. I just really enjoy your company and think that we could have a lot of fun together," Luke said. "I guess that we had better head back. It's already 5:00 P.M. I know that both of us have an early day tomorrow. By the time we get back to the marina and unload, it will be close to six," Luke said and turned and walked back to the front of the boat. Madison felt about two inches tall for dreaming of one man while kissing another. This didn't make any sense. She was dreaming of a man that she never met, and she pushed away a really great guy. *How am I going to fix this?* she asked herself. When Madison gathered up her belongings and took the courage to walk up to the top deck, Luke was there standing driving the boat toward the marina.

"Hi." Madison paused and then took a step forward until she was just beside Luke. "I hope that you aren't mad at me. I really did enjoy this afternoon. I hope that maybe we can do it again once I have my conference over with," Madison said and then sat down in the passenger chair. They continued the drive in somewhat silence before Luke finally spoke.

"I really like you, Madison. I enjoy spending time with you, and I would like to see where this can go. If you want to, that is. But I want to take it as slow as you need. I'm in no big hurry," Luke said and then smiled at Madison.

"I would like to think about that, Luke, but I really did enjoy today. I had a lot of fun. Thank you," Madison said.

"Think as long as you need," Luke replied and winked at Madison.

He really does have a great smile and is really hot, Madison thought. They rode the rest of the way in silence. About twenty minutes later, they pulled into the marina. They unloaded the boat and took everything to the SUV. Madison got her bag and grabbed her book that she hadn't even gotten the chance to read. They both got in and started toward Madison's house.

As they pulled into her driveway, Madison looked over at Luke and paused and then stated, "Would you like to stay for dinner?" She really didn't know if she wanted him to stay but just didn't want to end this day on bad terms.

"I would love to, but I think that I'll pass tonight. I have an early day, and I know that you have some paperwork to get started. I appreciate the offer," Luke said and leaned over and gave her a peck on the cheek.

"Okay, but I insist on a rain check," Madison said while stepping out of the SUV and gathering up her bag.

"Okay. I'll call you later," Luke said.

"Okay," Madison replied. She closed the door and started up to her front door. She glanced back and saw that Luke was making sure that she got into the house safely. He really was a gentleman. Madison stepped inside her house and then peeked out the window as Luke was backing out of her driveway. She wondered if she would ever see him again. She wondered if she would ever get over the fact that while she was kissing Luke she wanted it to be her sexy wrecker driver.

The next week went by so fast that Madison didn't know what was going on. She had been getting ready for her upcoming conference by making sure that the samples and brochures were ready. She felt confident that the subject she was going to teach on would leave an everlasting impression on her and her business. Today was Monday, and the conference was Tuesday, Wednesday, Thursday, and Friday. Luke had called twice this week, and Madison had talked briefly with him. She was grateful that he understood how busy she was and that she really didn't have time for anything else other than work. The conference was going to start tomorrow. Madison felt as though now that everything was in place, she could somewhat relax. She got up from her desk and went into Megan's office.

"Mom, are you busy this afternoon?" Madison asked.

"No, I don't think so. I think that everything that can be prepared is prepared. We've all worked extremely hard over this last week. I was just sitting here taking a breather," Megan replied.

"Well, the reason that I'm asking is that the conference has a black tie affair the last evening. You're my date, so to speak, and we need to go shopping for an evening dress. Are you up for the challenge of shopping?" Madison said and winked at her mom.

"Oh, I think that I can handle it. Let's go," Megan said as she got up and reached for her purse.

Madison and Megan both got their things together. They told the staff to make sure that all of the materials got sent over to the conference room and put up so that they could have access to them easily. Over the next two hours, both mother and daughter shopped and shopped and shopped. Finally, they both picked out an evening dress. Madison picked a solid black strapless dress with a plunging neckline, and the hem of the dress came just to her knees. Megan picked a navy dress that was floor length. They both bought necklaces and earrings to match. After lugging their packages around, they decided that they were hungry and stopped in the mall's food court. While they ate, they talked about the conference and what was expected. Both knew that the Trent Design seminar was going to be awesome.

"Madison, I just want you to know that I'm so proud of you. I know beyond a shadow of a doubt that this conference will be great. *You* will be great," Megan said and placed her hand on top of her daughter's.

"Thank you, Mom. I couldn't have done all of this without you. I appreciate all of the hard work that you do with and for me," Madison responded and leaned over and kissed her mom on the cheek. "I love you, Mom."

"I love you too," Megan said. Madison noticed hat her mom's bright green eyes were watering up. Megan was getting more emotional the older she got. Madison suspected that she missed Madison's dad more than she let on. The two women got up and retrieved their bags. They walked out to the parking lot and got in Madison's SUV. Madison glanced down at her watch and noticed that it was already six thirty.

"Wow, this day has flown by. I will drop you off at the office so that you can get your car. In the morning, I can pick you up at home if you would like to ride with me to the conference," Madison said as they pulled into the office parking lot.

"Sure, that sounds great. You know that I hate to fight the traffic and parking. What time will you be by to pick me up?" Megan asked.

"I will pick you up at seven. The conference starts at nine, but I want to leave early to make sure that we get a good parking place and that everything is where it is supposed to be," Madison responded.

"Okay, I'll be ready. Madison, don't worry. This conference will be great." "I know." Madison watched as her mom got out, walked to her car, got in, and started to back out of the parking lot. One thing that worried Madison was that her mom didn't waste any time driving. She got in her car, and off she went. Madison drove the rest of the way home in silence. She knew that this week was going to be loud, and she wanted to savor this quiet time. Friday evening was the black tie affair, and Madison was excited. She hadn't had any reason to get all dressed up in quite a while. Madison was teaching on Wednesday morning and then again on Thursday morning. She was attending classes with her staff all day on Tuesday and then again on Friday morning. She had purposely not scheduled anything for Friday afternoon because she wanted to come home and get ready and not feel as though she had to rush around.

Madison pulled into her driveway and unloaded her SUV. After setting her packages on the kitchen table, she stood there for a moment and took a deep breath. She was tired and kind of lonely. She decided that she would take an early bath and maybe read her book. She stepped into her bathroom, thinking that a nice, long, hot bath would help to relieve the tension in her body and maybe relax her. She sat in the tub for about thirty minutes and maybe only read three pages of her book.

While she soaked in the tub, she decided to say a small prayer. "Dear God, thank you for everything that you have blessed me with. Thank you for blessing me with my talent. I ask that you be with me as I teach and that I learn things along the way. Oh, and maybe you could arrange for me to see my mystery wrecker driver again. Thank you again, and forgive me of all my sins. Amen." Madison smiled and felt the peace wash over her. She was so thankful for her faith. It got her through her days and kept her strong to deal with anything. Madison got out and put on her nightgown. She crawled into bed, pulled the covers up, and within ten minutes she was fast asleep.

* * *

Tuesday morning was just as Madison expected: busy and full of people all looking somewhat lost. Madison had picked up her mom a few minutes before seven, and they got to the conference building with no problems. Madison slept so soundly that she almost didn't hear the alarm going off that morning. But Tuesday was good; all of her staff arrived at eight, and were all excited about what they would be hearing in the seminar. They arrived early to get a good seat and to see what other vendors were doing. Madison had arranged to have lunch ready for her staff at a nearby restaurant. That was the least that Madison could do. She enjoyed her staff, and they all worked extremely hard for her. She had only brought seven of her staff with her to this conference. She chose the seven based on work and seniority. The seven people had all been with Trent Design for over five years, and they knew the ins and outs of being in design. The nine of them, with Madison and her mom included, sat down and listened to the morning's seminar on color techniques. The afternoon class was also on other color techniques. They all seemed to really enjoy it, but they were ready to go when the day was finished.

Madison dropped her mom off at her house and then went home. She wanted to go over the material that she was going to be teaching. Madison enjoyed teaching and sharing with others what she did for a living; but she was also smart enough not to give away all of her trade secrets. She didn't want everyone as good as Trent Design. People came from all over, not only designers, but also ordinary people who just wanted tips on how to redecorate their homes or offices. The ordinary people were whom Madison enjoyed the most. She liked to let them know how they could redo something simple and not that expensive, but if they wanted a complete makeover for their home or office, she wanted them to be impressed with Trent Design, and give her a call. She wanted it all.

While Madison ate her dinner, she reviewed her notes and felt confident that she would give a great presentation. She cleaned up the kitchen and then decided that she would watch TV just for a little while. After all, it was already eight o'clock, and she knew that she needed her rest in order to give her all while teaching.

While Madison lay on her bed watching a rerun of *Golden Girls,* she thought back to her life and the things that she still wanted to accomplish. She wanted to get married. She wanted kids. And most importantly, she wanted her family to go to church and have a plan of action and a plan of faith. She nodded off, and when she woke back up, she rolled over and noticed that it was already 10:30 P.M. She turned off the TV and light and snuggled down into her bed, thinking about what she would say tomorrow in her presentation.

Zachary woke up on Wednesday morning and crawled out of bed. He had taken the day off to attend the seminar on redecorating. He had been wanting to redecorate for some time but had never seen any companies' samples that he really liked enough to hire them. Zachary didn't want to go to this alone, so he was taking his cousin Ann. She had always had an eye for taste and what looked good and what didn't. He had picked up a brochure and had noticed that a company named Trent Design was giving this seminar. He was first impressed due to the fact that the owner wasn't only going to teach the seminar, but he found out that she actually went to a lot of the jobs and assisted in them herself. He admired that. Most big wigs these days made other people do all of the grunt work, but not Trent Design. As he jumped in the shower, he thought ahead to his busy week. Granted, it was halfway over, but he still had to work some. He had left the company in good hands, and he had handed out all the assignments and told the men to get to it and bring in some vehicles. Zachary was proud of his company, very proud of it. He thought back, and from last Wednesday to yesterday, his company had repossessed thirty-four vehicles. That was a great six days.

After jumping in the shower and getting dressed, he made a quick call to the office. He talked with the secretary, Maxine, who assured him that everything was in good hands. Maxine was so reliable. When she knew that Zachary wasn't going to be in the office, she always made sure that she arrived at the office at eight to start fielding any calls from clients who might want an update on a particular vehicle that they had out for repossession.

Zachary knew that he could relax and enjoy his day and hopefully find someone who he could hire to redecorate his house, or find something he could do himself. As Zachary drove toward Ann's house, he looked down at his watch, and it was already 8:25. He didn't know where the time had gone, but he had to get a move on it. He sped up and pulled into Ann's driveway at 8:35. Ann was waiting on him at the door.

"Where have you been? You're late," Ann said as she slid into the passenger seat. "Sorry. I thought that I was on time, but I guess when I called the office, I talked a little longer than I thought. Hang on. I have to make up for lost time," Zachary said as he put his truck into gear and accelerated out onto the street.

"I hope that this seminar is good. I remember the last one that we went to. It was so boring. It seemed like all that company decorated was nursing homes," Ann said jokingly.

"I know what you mean. I think that this one will be good. Don't ask me why. I just have a feeling," Zachary said. They rode the rest of the way, talking about what had been going on in their lives. Ann was dating this man that she really wanted to marry. Zachary had met him and thought that he was great for Ann, but Ann was getting a little nervous the more serious the relationship got. They discussed Zachary's business and the fact that Zachary wasn't dating anyone. Ann thought that he was such a great catch. She couldn't figure out why some hot-blooded woman hadn't snagged him up yet. But Ann knew Zachary, and he was picky, sometimes a little too picky. Zachary knew what he wanted, and he wasn't going to settle for less. He wanted someone who was smart and could carry on a serious discussion with him or play around with him. He wanted someone who was cute and fun and not stuck on herself. He wanted someone to go to church with him; he wanted to start a family. Plus, he was ready to settle down. Zachary also wanted someone who worked and had a career. "Well, here we are," Zachary said as he pulled his truck into a parking space at the conference arena.

Zachary and Ann got out of the truck and started walking toward the conference doors. As they entered, they detoured toward the information table. They knew that they wanted the seminar with Trent Design. Zachary had done his homework and had found out that Trent Design was a well-known company and growing rapidly. Zachary paid for the admission for him and Ann, and they walked into the conference room. As they walked into the conference room, they noticed that most of the seats in the room were already taken. Apparently all of the other people had found out that Trent Design was a good company and did great work. Zachary and Ann found two seats toward the back of the room and sat down.

◦ ◦ ◦

Madison peeked out from behind the curtain and saw that the room was filling quickly. She had decided at the last moment to place tables and chairs in the room instead of just chairs. She decided that she would give people somewhere to write and take notes. Madison and her staff had also laid out samples and literature on the tables, so the seating and tables had been a great idea. Madison was getting somewhat nervous. She didn't really know why; she had given tons of conferences and knew she was used to this by now. She hoped that this seminar would boost her reputation, as well as get her some new clients. She knew that some of these people were just here to get ideas and that they couldn't afford to hire her and her company, but she didn't mind. She enjoyed helping people make their homes or offices a little more cheerful and happy. She knew quite a few designers that would take applications at the seminars. That way, those designers could pick and choose who would be able to pay for services. Madison wasn't like that. She was thankful for her business and just found that she had a way with colors and designs. She didn't mind helping out the "ordinary people," as some designers called them.

"Madison, are you ready?" Simon, one of her employees, asked. "Yes, I'm as ready as I'll ever be. I'm never nervous, but for some reason, I am today. What do you think is up with that?" Madison asked.

"I don't know, Madison," Simon said. "I've never seen you uptight about anything, especially about teaching a seminar; you've done this hundreds of times. You could probably do this in your sleep. Don't worry. You'll be great. Everything is set up and ready to go. I think that everyone out there is looking forward to hearing you and the ideas of Trent Design." Simon finished and gave Madison a wink and then looked at his watch. It was nine o'clock on the dot.

"Showtime," Madison said to herself as she took a deep breath and waited for Simon to go and greet the attendees of the seminar. Simon was always good at the introductions.

"Welcome to the Trent Design seminar. My name is Simon, and I'll be briefly giving you a history of Trent Design and our fearless leader, Madison Trent. So please sit back and relax. This is going to be a seminar that you will never forget," Simon said as he smiled widely.

Zachary listened as this Simon person talked about Trent Design. He was actually surprised but happy that Simon was going over all of the basics of this company. Whomever he hired, he wanted to know who he was hiring and what they stood for. Zachary listened and took some notes. He found out that Trent Design had been in business for eight years and that they were going big. They had recently just gotten a contract for a major office building for all of the lobbies on each floor and not to mention the offices on each floor. Simon went on to say that Trent Design was about the client. Trent Design would give ideas and samples, but ultimately it was the clients' decision on what they liked and wanted in their home or office. Zachary was really impressed with the stats and information he was finding out. Next, Simon started to introduce the owner and operator, Madison Trent. *Great,* Zachary thought, *some old lady with a million accomplishments.*

"Now, I will talk about and eventually introduce the owner, Madison Trent," Simon began. "Madison went to college in Texas, where she got a degree in interior design and business. She held top honors in each interior design class. She maintained a 4.0 grade point average throughout her college career. After college, she moved to Houston and started Trent Design. Back then, she only had a handful of employees, and now, eight years later, Trent Design has around twenty-two employees. Madison also teaches seminars all over Texas, Oklahoma, New Mexico, Colorado, and Nevada. When Madison isn't teaching a seminar, she is at the office, brainstorming on how to make better color schemes and samples. She enjoys being hands-on with a job. When she isn't teaching, she is always with us, helping to get the job finished with the satisfaction of the client. Madison Trent is the best teacher and interior designer that you will ever meet. She is creative and intriguing. So, without any further chatting from me, please join me in a warm welcome for Madison Trent, owner of Trent Design." Simon finished and smiled warmly, waiting for Madison to walk out and take over.

Madison stood behind the curtain and listened to Simon talk about her company and about her. Simon was getting really good at this. Madison took out her compact and lipstick and reapplied some color. She then checked her hose to make sure that she didn't have a run or snag anywhere. She finally tuned back in to Simon when she heard him say, "Please join me in a warm welcome for Madison Trent, owner of Trent Design." Madison took a deep breath, straightened her suit, and walked out onto the stage.

"Hello and good morning. I'm Madison Trent. I thank each and every one of you for taking time out of your busy schedules to come and attend this seminar. Please feel free to take notes and feel and observe the samples and brochures at each table. I hope that I can give each and every one of you an idea to take back with you to your home or office to give it just a little face lift." Madison finished and smiled. *Wow,* she thought, *this room is full. There has to be at least two hundred people here. Maybe some of these will be clients one day.* She paused and then got out her notes and itinerary, looking up at all the faces looking her over. *This is great,* she thought. *This is where I always wanted to be.*

Zachary Mann couldn't see who had just walked out on the stage. The person that was sitting in front of him had a huge head. Zachary moved his chair a little so that he could see, but he was having a hard time. Finally, he looked at Ann and asked her to scoot her chair over some so that he could move his chair. He could hear the woman speaking and knew that surely she couldn't be that old; she had a great voice. After finally getting his chair where he could see, he got out his pen and took one of the brochures and opened it up. *Okay,* he thought, *I'm ready to learn and get some ideas.* Maybe if he liked this company, he would hire them to come and redecorate this house. Zachary looked up and found his way to the stage, where he saw her, the woman of his dreams. Madison Trent was the woman that he had seen for the last couple of weeks, the goddess of his life. Zachary felt himself getting restless and shifted in his chair. *Wow,* he thought. He was going to talk to Madison Trent. He would just have to find a way how and where. Zachary had found his soul mate.

Zachary couldn't believe his eyes. Standing on the stage, only about thirty feet in front of him, was Madison Trent. Madison was the woman who he had been dreaming about for the last two weeks. He couldn't believe his luck. Now he knew who and what company he was going to hire to redecorate his home and hopefully his life. Zachary had to stop thinking like that. He hadn't even talked to Madison yet, but he was bound and determined to by Friday night. *That's it,* he thought. He would introduce himself and his proposal to redecorate his home on Friday night at the black tie dinner. He really had to make sure that he looked perfect. He couldn't wait until that moment when they met. He just hoped that Madison would feel the fireworks as much as he did just looking at her.

"Zachary, are you all right?" His cousin Ann interrupted his thoughts.

"Yes, I'm fine. Why do you ask?" Zachary asked.

"Well, you kind of look like you have seen a ghost. Are you feeling all right?" Ann asked again.

"Yes, I feel great. I just didn't think that this Madison Trent person would be so young. I was thinking of hiring her company to redecorate my home. I guess that I'll have to listen to her today and then determine if this company is the right one for me," Zachary said, hoping that he didn't draw any attention to himself. Ann was pretty smart, but Zachary didn't want her to know that Madison was the woman of his dreams.

"Okay then. Pay attention and listen to her. She sounds like she knows what she is talking about," Ann pointed out.

Zachary sat there for the morning session really not listening, just looking and watching the beautiful Madison Trent. She was graceful and had perfect posture, he noticed. Her voice was soothing and comforting. Zachary really didn't care how expensive her company was. He had to have her, and he wanted her now more than he imagined. He wanted to marry her. Zachary wasn't the type to kiss and tell, that was for sure, and he wasn't the type for a one-night stand. He wanted something different. He wanted a meaningful relationship with someone who was in love with him as much as he was with her. He wanted a partner. He wanted someone to pray with, play with, and grow old with. His parents had that type of relationship; they always prayed together. They spent time together and really truly enjoyed each other's company. They were best friends and had put God first in their lives from the very beginning, and that is what Zachary wanted. Zachary was ready for it all. He wanted to settle down. He wanted Madison Trent.

Madison looked around the room as she spoke. She always tried to make it a point to look each and every person in the eye. Eye contact was very important, she heard her father saying. As Madison went from one person to the other, she realized that almost every person in the room was taking notes and looking at the samples provided. Madison hoped that some of these people would be calling her. Madison had worked long and hard for this and was enjoying her life.

As she continued to look around the room, Madison thought back to her dad. He was a great man, and she loved him very much. She knew that beyond a shadow of a doubt that her dad would be so proud of her today. She missed him so much, but she tried really hard not to think about him. Madison turned all of her attention back to her mission to get clients.

Madison spent the next three hours going over color techniques and samples and giving ideas to the people that possibly couldn't afford to hire a decorator. By the end of the seminar, at 4:00 P.M., Madison was exhausted, but her mind was still spinning around and around in her head. About half of the seminar people hung out after the class to talk to Madison and to meet her. She almost felt like a celebrity. After all was said and done and everyone one had left but Madison and her staff, they all cleaned up and then headed home.

"Madison?" Megan said.

"Yeah, Mom, what's up?" Madison asked.

"Nothing, I just wanted you to know that you gave an excellent seminar. I think that you gave a lot of ideas, and I just know that you'll get calls from this. Would you like to go and grab a bite to eat?"

"Thank you. I hope that we get some calls. Yeah, we can go and get a bite to eat. Where would you like to go?" Madison asked.

Over the next two hours, Megan and Madison sat outside at the café around the corner. They talked and laughed. Madison was thankful that she and her mother could talk and confide in each other. After the luncheon, Madison decided that she was going to go home and take a short nap.

* * *

Madison woke up on Friday morning and wondered where the week went. This was the last day of the conference, and she and her staff were going to a half-day class. She was excited but a bit tired. This week had accomplished a lot. Her staff had thoroughly enjoyed themselves and got a new perspective on things. They were all pumped up and ready to work and get some new jobs. Madison joined her mother and her staff for the seminar on painting and wallpapering. Madison personally didn't like wallpapering much, she preferred painting.

All afternoon, Madison kept daydreaming about the wrecker driver. She hadn't seen him or any truck that resembled Mann Co. She thought that it was probably for the best. She didn't even know his name, and she figured that he was either married or had a girlfriend or one of each. She knew that someone was out there for her. She just wanted to find him.

"Madison?" Simon asked, poking her on the shoulder.

"What?" Madison turned her head and looked at Simon.

"It's time to go. The seminar is over. Where are you? You have been daydreaming all afternoon," Simon answered.

"Oh, sorry. I just have a lot of things on my mind," Madison replied. She didn't want her staff to know that she was daydreaming of the wrecker driver and that it had nothing to do with work.

She wondered what his hand would feel like holding her hand. She wondered what his lips would feel like if she ever got the chance to kiss him. She wondered everything about him. He was beautiful, and she wanted to find him. Madison gathered up her purse and notes and placed them in her briefcase. She was ready to go home and get herself pampered for tonight's dinner party. She walked out to her SUV and yelled back at her mom that she would pick her up at six. The party didn't start until seven. Madison got in her SUV and started home. She wanted to take a nice long bath and put a couple of cucumbers on her eyes; she noticed that they were a bit puffy this morning when she woke up. Thirty minutes later, Madison settled down in a long tub with fresh cucumber slices on her eyes. She was excited about tonight and wanted it to be memorable.

Zachary was at the office early on Friday morning. Maxine looked up at him as he walked through the door.

"Well, well. What brings the boss man in this early?" Maxine prodded.

"Nothing. I'm going to take half of the day off, and I wanted to get some work done. Any accounts come in this morning or last night?" Zachary asked.

"Yes, you had six new accounts. I have already placed them in the computers and printed out the paperwork. The accounts are on your desk. Toby is already out this morning; he came by about thirty minutes ago, and I gave him three of the new accounts. I hope that was all right," Maxine explained.

"Yes, that's fine. Toby is a great employee, and he knows how to get the job done. You know that I trust your judgment," Zachary answered and sat down at his desk. He didn't sleep very well last night, or the night before, for that matter. He couldn't get Madison Trent out of his mind. He had done his homework on her. She wasn't married, and she had never been. That was enough information for him. He wanted to meet her, and tonight was the night.

Zachary had already made up his mind that he was leaving the office around one. He wanted to go home and maybe take a nap and take his time getting dressed. His first stop on the way home was to pick up his tux.

"Zachary, you have a call on line one," Maxine said, interrupting Zachary's thoughts.

"Hello? Okay. Thank you. I will pick it up around noon," Zachary said as he hung up the phone. Maxine didn't know who he was talking to; she could only hear her side of the conversation. Zachary looked up at Maxine and smiled.

"My tuxedo is ready. I'm going to that black tie dinner tonight. Remember, I told you about it." Zachary paused and looked at his long time secretary.

"Oh, I remember you saying something about it. Are you taking a date? If not, I'm sure that I can set you up with someone," Maxine stated, being somewhat nosy.

"You stop it right there. I don't need a date. I'm going with Ann. So don't get any ideas on trying to set me up," Zachary said as he winked at Maxine and turned his attention back to his computer.

Zachary knew that Maxine was always trying to set him up with someone, but tonight he was going to meet someone himself. Zachary continued working, or at least he tried. He couldn't keep his mind on his work. Tonight was the night that was hopefully going to change the rest of his life. Zachary glanced down at his watch, and it only read ten thirty. *Oh well,* he thought. *I will just go ahead and get some paperwork together and leave earlier than I expected.* Thirty minutes later, Zachary was picking up his keys and heading for the front door.

"Bye, Maxine. I'll see you on Monday. Have a great weekend," Zachary said and shut the door behind him.

"Bye. Have a good time tonight," Maxine said.

Zachary got in his truck and headed to pick up his tuxedo. He wanted to go ahead and try it on to make sure that it fit just perfect. At 1 p.m., Zachary was pulling into his driveway and ready to go and try to take a nap to get Madison Trent out of his head. He didn't think that it would work, but he would try. He was going to figure out what he was going to say to her when he met her. He wanted it to be perfect.

* * *

Madison Trent lay on her bed, relaxing, when she looked over at the clock and it already read 4 p.m. *Wow,* she thought, *where has all of the day gone to?* After she got out of her bath, she lay down, and laid the cucumbers back on her eyes, and listened to music. She must have dozed off. Now, after she woke up, the cucumbers were on the side of the bed and the CD that she put in had stopped. Madison got up and started toward her closet. She had bought a special dress just for this occasion, and she was excited. She wanted tonight to be perfect. Just then, dragging her from her thoughts, the phone rang.

"Hello?" Madison answered.

"Hey, what are you doing?" Abigail asked.

"Nothing really. I just woke up from a nap and was going to start getting my clothes out for tonight. I am really excited," Madison replied.

"Oh, yeah. I forgot about the dinner tonight. Mark and I were going to dinner and thought that maybe we could double date with you and Luke," Abigail stated.

"Oh my goodness. Luke called the office earlier in the week, and I totally forgot to call him back. This week has been crazy. I'll try to call him before I leave for the dinner. Maybe we can get together tomorrow or something," Madison said.

"Well, maybe tomorrow, if you are still in Luke's good graces, we can all go out on his huge boat and have a lot of fun in the sun. Anyway, I hope that you have a good time tonight. If you want, you can call me in the morning," Abigail said.

"Thank you. I'll call you in the morning. I'll let you go so I can try to call Luke real quick. Do you think that I can reach him at the office?" Madison asked.

"I think that I would call Luke on his cell phone. I'll talk to you later," Abigail said and hung up the phone.

Madison put the phone down and headed to the bathroom to start applying her makeup. She told her mother that she would pick her at 6 p.m. First, though, she would try to call Luke. She got her planner from the kitchen table to get Luke's cell phone number. She fumbled through the pages, finally finding where she put it. She picked up the phone and noticed that she was nervous. Luke was a great guy, and she thought that she owed him by calling him back. He was a gentleman and knew how to treat a woman. After all, she didn't have a steady boyfriend, and Luke was gorgeous. She carefully dialed his number and listened to the phone ring about three times, and then a deep voice answered.

"Hello?" Luke said.

"Hi, it's Madison. First let me just tell you that I'm really sorry that I didn't return your call this week. I've been in conferences all week, and I totally forgot. How are you?" Madison asked, trying not to sound like she was giddy or nervous, both of which she felt.

"Hey!" Luke replied, so happy that she had called him back. "I was thinking about you earlier in the week, so I thought that I would call. I forgot that you were in the conferences. I'm good. I wish that we could get together. Maybe for dinner, or what about a boat outing? I really had fun the other time we went." Luke paused, thinking to himself that he sounded like a fool chatting away so much.

"Well, I already have plans tonight, but maybe tomorrow afternoon we could get together. Abigail called earlier and wanted to know if we all wanted to go out, but she forgot that I already had plans for tonight," Madison said, feeling somewhat happy inside.

Luke smiled. This woman was smart and a challenge to boot. He was going to get her somehow.

"Hey, I have an idea. Why don't the four of us get together tomorrow afternoon? I will talk with Mark and Abigail and see what they want to do. Why don't you call me tomorrow about noon?" Luke paused, waiting for Madison's answer.

"That sounds good. I'll call you tomorrow. Thanks for not being upset with me that it took me all week to get back with you," Madison said smoothly.

"No problem. I know that you're a busy woman. I admire that. I'll talk to you tomorrow. Have a good evening," Luke said.

Madison hung up the phone and sat there somewhat amazed that Luke wasn't the least bit jealous or curious of what she was going to be doing tonight. She liked that but thought that maybe Luke had other ideas of playing hard to get. Madison still felt bad about the kiss that they shared. After all, she was thinking of the wrecker driver.

At exactly 5:45, she hated being late, Madison pulled into her mother's driveway. Megan was waiting with a glass of Coke in her hand.

"Wow!" Madison said. "Mom, you look amazing. We should attend these more often." Madison gave her mom a wink.

"Thank you, dear. You look beautiful. That dress fits you perfectly. You'll turn every man's head tonight," Megan stated. "Would you like a drink before we leave?" Megan asked.

"Yeah, that sounds good. What do you have?" Madison asked.

"I'm not sure. Look in the fridge," Megan said while she finished gathering up her purse and reapplying some lipstick and perfume.

Madison turned and walked into the kitchen. This was the house that she grew up in, and she knew it like the back of her hand. She loved this house. It brought back so many memories. She opened the fridge and reached for a Diet Coke from the back and then turned and started walking toward the front room where Megan was waiting for her.

"Are you ready to go?" Madison asked her mom.

"Yes, this is as good as it is going to get," Megan said with a slight laugh.

"Okay, let's go. I'm starving," Madison responded as she carried out her Diet Coke to the SUV.

Twenty minutes later, they were pulling into the parking lot and were surprised to see all of the people there already. Madison and Megan were a good thirty minutes early before the dinner and entertainment even began, but the parking lot was already pretty full. Madison pulled up to the line for the valet parking. She wasn't going to walk all over this parking lot in this evening gown, so she was going to enjoy this evening and take advantage of all of the luxuries that it offered. Madison glanced down to her watch and noticed that they had been waiting in line a full five minutes. She didn't know where the time had gone. She must have been daydreaming, and apparently so had her mom. She had barely said two words since they left the house.

"Mom, are you okay? You're really quiet tonight," Madison asked carefully as she pulled up in line. She was the next vehicle, and she was grateful.

"I'm fine. I guess that I'm just thinking back," Megan answered and looked at her daughter. Madison was all grown up now and was undeniably radiant. Megan could see her late husband in her daughter, and it made her smile, but in the same respect made her heart hurt. She loved him and always would. Always.

"Anything that you want to talk about?" Madison asked as she rolled down her window.

"No, not right now," Megan answered, smiling.

"Okay, Mom. It's time," Madison said and put her SUV in park and reached to get her purse. The valet attendant opened the door for her.

"Thank you," Madison stated while exchanging her parking ticket for a ten-dollar bill that she tipped the attendant.

"Thank you, ma'am. Hope you have an incredible evening," the attendant answered.

Madison had this feeling that this evening was going to change her life. She couldn't figure out why she felt this way. She just had this feeling that wouldn't go away. She knew that she was definitely up for the challenge of whatever tonight brought her way.

Zachary Mann had just finished buttoning his cuff links when the phone rang.

"Hello?" Zachary asked.

"Zachary? Is that you?" Ann asked.

"Yep, Ann what's wrong?" Zachary questioned her.

"I don't know what happened. I felt fine yesterday and this morning, but about three hours ago, I started getting sick. I thought that it would go away, but it hasn't. I'm afraid that I can't go with you tonight to the interior design dinner. I'm so sorry."

"That's okay. I'll try to get a hold of someone else to go. I'm sorry that you are sick. Is there anything that I can do for you?" Zachary asked. He could tell in his cousin's voice that she was sick. Besides, Ann wasn't the type of person who would try to get out of something.

"No, I'm fine. Just go ahead tonight and have a great time. I'll call you tomorrow to see how it went," Ann said.

"Okay. I hope you feel better. Bye," Zachary said and sat the phone in his lap. Where was he going to find a replacement that would have a tux or an evening gown on hand? After all, the dinner started in an hour. Zachary sat there and started to brainstorm who would be able to go with him on such short notice. He really didn't want to take one of his guy friends with him; he would prefer to take a woman. *Hold on,* he thought. He would call Maxine. She used to go to all kinds of dinner functions. Surely she would have something that she could wear. He only hoped that she didn't have any plans tonight. He picked up her phone and dialed the number that he had memorized years before.

"Hello?" Maxine answered.

"Max, it's Zachary. I'm glad that you're home. Are you busy tonight?" Zachary asked.

"No, not really. Just relaxing after a busy day. Why? What's up?" Maxine asked. She thought the world of Zachary. Not only was he her boss, but he was her friend, almost like a child to her. He was so sweet and caring.

"Well," Zachary began, "Ann called and is sick, and I don't have a date for tonight. I was wondering if you still had a few of those fancy dresses and felt like attending with me." Zachary paused, giving Maxine time to ponder her answer.

"Sure, Zachary," Maxine stated. "It would be really fun to go with you. I only need about fifteen minutes to get ready. I'm sorry about Ann, but I'm just delighted that you asked me to go with you. You're such a handsome man, Zachary. I'm flattered that you called this old woman to go. I'll see you in just a few minutes," Maxine finished, hanging up the phone and leaving Zachary listening to a dial tone.

He was grateful for Maxine. She had always been there for him, giving advice and listening to him. Twenty minutes later, Zachary was ringing the doorbell to Maxine's house. Maxine opened the door and smiled, inviting Zachary inside.

"Wow, you look wonderful," Zachary said while walking in the door.

"What? You think that just because I'm old enough to be your grandma that I don't know how to get dressed up? Well, you're wrong. I still know how to have a good time. Now, come on. We don't want to be late," Maxine said with a wink as she picked up her purse.

While driving across town to the dinner, Maxine and Zachary talked about all kinds of things. Zachary really did have a lot of faith in this woman. She was smart and always had a huge heart, always ready to help him. They arrived, and Zachary pulled up to the valet parking line and waited his turn, which was only one car. He handed the keys to the attendant and got out, sliding the attendant a tip. Zachary then walked to the other side where Maxine was standing. The attendant had already helped her out of the truck. Zachary held out his arm, and Maxine took it proudly. Zachary had two things on his mind tonight. One was to meet Madison Trent, and the second was to get her to redecorate his house and hopefully his heart. He didn't want her company to do the work; he wanted her to do it. He didn't care how long it took or what the cost. He wanted Madison Trent, and he wanted her bad. He smiled and patted Maxine's hand, and they went to check in and see where their table was. Zachary knew that Madison Trent was sitting at the front table. He had done his homework, but what he didn't know yet was how that he was going to introduce himself and how he was going to talk her into working on his house.

"Zachary, you look like the cat that ate the mouse," Maxine said with a slight pat on the arm. "What are you thinking about?"

"Nothing really. Just wondering who I'm going to hire to redecorate my house. I have a company in mind. I just need to figure out how to get them to agree," Zachary said while feeling his cheeks blushing.

"Well, by the looks of you, I would say that it is a woman. Am I right?" Maxine pressed.

"Oh, Maxine. You are always up to your matchmaking. Just enjoy your night," Zachary said while reaching in his pocket and pulling out the tickets.

"Good evening. Welcome to the design dinner. You are both at table five. Enjoy your evening," the attractive brunette said while looking Zachary over.

"Thank you. We will," Zachary replied, not giving the poor woman any attention whatsoever. He couldn't believe his luck. He was sitting at table five, just four tables away from the woman of his dreams. How perfect was this? Now all he had to decide was when he was going to meet her. Should he do it before dinner or after? He really didn't know what to do. He led Maxine to their table, all the while looking for Madison. He didn't see her, but he knew that she was here; he could feel it.

* * *

Madison was talking with a rich future client when she noticed that her pulse was starting to race and her stomach was flipping with butterflies, lots of butterflies. *What is all of this about?* she thought. She didn't have any feelings about this client. She knew that for sure. She looked over at her mom, Megan, and smiled.

"Honey, are you all right? You look a little flushed," Megan asked, concerned for her daughter. Megan knew that Madison had put a lot of hours in lately and didn't want her to overdo it.

"I feel fine. I think that I just need some fresh air. Would you please excuse me? Please call my office, and we will set up a formal appointment to discuss all of your decoration needs." Madison gave her best business smile and shook hands with the prospective clients. She then walked toward the patio at the end of the room and stepped just outside the door. She didn't know what she was feeling, but it felt like someone had entered the room, someone that she didn't know but wanted to. She didn't know what was going on. *Maybe I'm losing it,* she thought.

Right then, while she was still thinking about feeling lightheaded and the butterflies fluttering in her stomach, the president of the design conference announced that dinner would be served in five minutes and to please find your way to your table. Madison sucked in a breath and walked proudly to her table, all the while pausing to shake hands and make small talk with potential clients. Madison finally sat down beside Megan.

"I feel better. I think that I just needed a bit of fresh air," Madison replied before her mother could ask her any questions. Madison was thankful that she had chosen to bring her mother. Megan deserved it, and Madison knew that she could always depend on her mother. They had been through a lot together, and they shared a very special bond, one that would never go away.

"Ladies and gentleman," she heard as the director, Winston Bradford, was on stage, urging everyone to settle down and take their seats. "I would personally like to welcome each and every one of you for attending this year's conference and dinner. It is a great honor for me to be here tonight. We have a wonderful dinner prepared and dancing afterward. Before we start serving, I would like to introduce the two head tables." Mr. Bradford paused, giving everyone time to get quiet.

He started at the other table, for which Madison was happy. But he was quickly to her table, and Madison was nervous. She didn't know why, but she was.

"At the next table," Mr. Bradford continued, "we have a very special person. Not only did she teach at this year's conference, but she is one the most talented interior designers that you will ever meet. Shortly, she will be taking over the interior design world, so if you get time, and I urge you to, come and say hi to her if you have any decoration needs. Please welcome Madison Trent." Mr. Bradford paused, giving Madison time to stand up and turn around. She smiled and waved while everyone was clapping at her. She was flattered that Mr. Bradford would say anything like that. She definitely knew that tonight was going to be a busy night. Madison sat down, and the introductions were continued around the table. After all of the introductions were completed, the servers started going around to each table, asking what everyone would like to drink. Madison decided that she would have a red wine tonight. After all, the tickets for this dinner were over a hundred dollars a person. The ticket did give you one drink. Even though Madison didn't have to pay for her ticket, she was going to take advantage of it. She smiled while everyone else ordered drinks. Madison was looking around at everyone, trying to see if she could see any of her staff there. Madison was looking around table seven when she saw Noah and Dylan from her newest and largest account so far. Dylan was walking her way.

"Hi, Madison. You look amazing tonight. I was sorry that you didn't call me for dinner. But promise that you will save me a dance," Dylan said while laying a gentle kiss on Madison's cheek.

"Hello, Dylan. How have you been? I'm sorry that I didn't call. I have been extremely busy with this conference. Please accept my apology, and yes, I'll save you a dance." Madison smiled while inside cringing at the thought of having Dylan's hands anywhere on her body.

"You're on," Dylan said and then walked back toward his table. Maybe if he were lucky tonight, he could get Madison Trent, super interior girl, in his bed. He had high hopes.

Dinner was wonderful, Madison thought, sitting there with a full stomach from the lobster tail and London broil served along with fresh steamed vegetables and a baked potato. The dessert was coming up, and Madison didn't know if she could pull this off, but when the server sat it down in front of her, she knew that she could find a place. She took a bite of the strawberry tart; it was divine. Madison sat there and looked around, trying to figure out how she was going to get out of dancing with Dylan. She liked him as a client, but she didn't have any romantic interest in him at all. Ten minutes later, the servers were at the table taking dishes and asking if anyone would like another drink. Madison politely asked for a glass of water; she felt as though she would need it. Madison decided that she would get up and start to mingle. The dinner conversation was somewhat stuffy and boring at her table. All anyone wanted to talk about was what designs were in style and color schemes. Madison was tired of talking shop and wanted to relax and enjoy her evening.

Madison leaned toward Megan. "Mom, I'm going to mingle. I'll be back in a little while."

"Okay, have fun, honey," Megan said with a wink.

She knew that there were plenty of men nearby who thought that Madison was beautiful and couldn't wait to dance with her. Megan just didn't know if Madison would dance with them. *She can be quite stubborn,* Megan thought with a little laugh.

Madison got up and started toward a group of people who she knew from other conferences. She was talking with them when Dylan walked up.

"Are you ready for that dance?" Dylan asked.

"Ready as I'll ever be," Madison answered, hoping that Dylan didn't catch the sarcasm in her voice.

Dylan led her toward the dance floor. Madison paused long enough to place her glass on her table. When they reached the dance floor, a slow song started. Madison thought that the song would never end. *Dylan probably paid to have them play a slow song,* she thought. Dylan gathered her up in him arms and led her across the dance floor. Madison was trying hard not to let any part of her body come in contact with Dylan's. This was the last person she wanted to dance with. Granted, she was grateful that he was in the meeting a few weeks ago. Because of him and Noah, she got the huge deal, but she didn't intend for Dylan to be so forward and act like all he wanted was to try to make the moves on her. She wasn't that type of woman. Finally the song ended, and Dylan reluctantly let her out of his arms.

"You know something, Madison?" Dylan asked.

"No, what?" Madison responded, wondering what he was going to say.

"You feel like you belong in my arms. We seem to fit good together. What do you say we leave and go back to my house where we can visit and relax?" Dylan proposed, hoping he had a chance with her.

"I don't think so, Dylan. You know that I don't like to mix business and pleasure. Besides, I brought my mom tonight, and I just can't leave her. Thank you for the invitation, though. It was a sweet gesture. Excuse me. I have to go to the ladies' room," Madison said while pulling out from his grasp.

"Okay, whatever you say. You don't know what you are missing," Dylan responded. He let go of her and walked off the floor.

Madison didn't want to make him mad, but she didn't feel anything for Dylan. Madison made her way toward the patio and stopped at the bar to get another glass of water. After Dylan, she felt as though she needed some air. Madison reached the patio and noticed no one was out there. *Good,* she thought, *some peace and quiet.* Madison sat down on the bench and listened to the night sounds and kind of wished that she were home in bed with a good book. She had met a lot of people, and they all wanted her to decorate their house or office; Madison had thankfully grabbed some business cards and stuck them in her purse. To her amazement, she had already passed out every card she had. *It's amazing,* she thought. *If every one of these clients call, Trent Designs will be busy for the rest of the year.*

"Excuse me, may I join you?" Zachary asked with two glasses of punch in his hands.

Great, Madison thought without turning around, *some guy's trying to talk to me.* She was tired but reminded herself that she was someone whom people wanted to talk to.

"Sure, please sit down," Madison said, turning her head slowly and then gasping. She couldn't believe who was standing five feet from her. Her wrecker driver. *What's he doing here?* she thought. He was absolutely ravishing—tall, tan, and beautiful. She didn't know what to say or think. In front of her was the man of her dreams. In person, he was breathtaking. He had on a black tux with his hair pulled back into a little pony tail. He smelled so yummy that all she wanted to do was breathe him in for a few minutes. His eyes seemed so bright, and she couldn't stop staring at them. He was positively the most dashing man she had ever seen. Luke was built and was hot, but this man in front of her blew that all to shreds. This man was confident with a hint of danger, and the smile almost made her fall out of her chair.

"I'm sorry. Please sit down," Madison said, trying to cover her surprise and embarrassment.

Zachary sat down and handed her the glass of punch. She was everything that he had ever imagined, even more. He couldn't believe that he had been studying her for the last two hours and was just now talking with her.

"Hi, I'm Zachary Mann. It's a pleasure to meet you." Zachary felt like an awkward teenager.

"Hi, I'm Madison Trent," Madison responded, feeling like her cheeks were on fire. Thankfully, it was somewhat dark on the patio. Madison knew at this moment that this was what this night was all about. She was finally meeting her wrecker driver. *Wait a minute,* she told herself. *He is just a wrecker driver.* What was he doing at this party? She looked up and met his eyes; they were beautiful, big, and deep blue.

"Nice to meet you Zachary. Are you enjoying yourself tonight?" Madison asked, wondering why she half-way sounded like a recording.

"Yes, I'm having a wonderful time. What about yourself?" Zachary asked. He was trying to figure out how he was going to keep this woman interested in conversation to figure out how he was going to make the proposal for her to come and redecorate his house. He had seen the men that had kept up with her all evening and thought that she was probably tired of all the games. He didn't have any games; he just knew that he wanted Madison Trent in his life and now had to figure out how.

"I'm having a great time. I'm a little tired. It has been a long evening," Madison said, wondering how it was possible that her mystery man was now standing in front of her, talking to her. Now she realized that she wanted to know everything about him, mostly to figure out if he was just a wrecker driver or something more. What was he doing here? *Stop it,* she told herself. She had to get it together.

"Ms. Trent?" Zachary started.

"Oh, please call me Madison," Madison interrupted.

"Okay, Madison. I know that this is going to sound crazy, but haven't we met before? I think I saw you the other morning at the stoplight around eight. Does that sound familiar?" Zachary paused, knowing full well that it was Madison Trent he saw that morning and the same Madison Trent he had been dreaming about for several weeks now.

Madison couldn't understand this. Was someone trying to play a cruel joke on her? Had he noticed her like she had noticed him? This was crazy.

"Yes, now that you mention it, I think I did see you the other day. I was running late and getting very impatient. I think that you were driving a wrecker? Am I correct?" Madison paused, hoping that he would go into detail about the wrecker.

"Yes, I had just finished picking up a car for repossession. I was on my way back to the office when I saw you. I thought you were in a bit of a hurry," Zachary replied. He was happy she had noticed him as well.

"Okay, Madison. I know that you don't know me and don't know what type of person I am, but I have a proposition for you." Zachary paused, wanting to see Madison's expression.

"Excuse me?" Madison asked, disappointed that he didn't go into an explanation about the wrecker. *Okay,* she thought, *the name on the wrecker said Mann Co., and this man just introduced himself as Zachary Mann.* Putting two and two together, she wondered if his dad or someone owned the company or if he did. She wasn't sure, but had to find out and soon.

"Please, just listen, Madison. I know a lot about your work and have watched you in your seminars, and you are exceptionally talented. I would like to hire you to come and redecorate my home."

"Mr. Mann," Madison started, trying to keep this somewhat professional.

"Call me Zachary," Zachary butted in.

"Okay, Zachary. I'll give you my office phone number, and we can set up an appointment so you and your wife can come in, and we can discuss all of your needs and wants, and we can see if we can come to some type of an agreement," Madison said sharply. She couldn't figure out why she was upset; after all, he only wanted to hire her. Here was the man of her dreams, and he wanted to hire her. *What is wrong with me?* she thought. *He's probably married anyhow.* She frowned, thinking that this man was completely out of her reach.

"Well, I was hoping that you would come and look at my home yourself. You see, I don't have a wife, and I don't really have a lot of time during the week in which I could make an appointment and meet with you." Zachary stopped and waited.

Madison couldn't believe her ears. This gorgeous man was not married. On top of that, he wanted her to come to his home, but then again, he was probably just wanting her to come over on a professional level, nothing else.

"Well, I usually have my staff come out and look and give you an estimate. I could have one of my employees come and meet you at your home." Madison paused, wondering what Zachary Mann was doing here and why he wanted her to come to his home.

"Okay, Madison, to be completely honest"—Zachary paused and looked directly into her eyes—"I want *you* to come and redecorate my home. I think that you are amazing and wonderful, and I want to work directly with you and you alone, no one else. I promise that I am not some weirdo. I will give you authorization to call around and ask people about me. I don't even care if you run a background check on me. I'm honest, and I want you." Zachary stopped and continued to look into her eyes. He didn't know if she would accept his offer or if she would tell him to go away.

Madison thought that her heart stopped. Had he

just told her that he wanted her and her alone? *Oh, stop it; he wants you only for redecorating his home, nothing else.* But was she dreaming? She still couldn't believe that this wrecker driver was at this expensive dinner. What was he doing here?

"If you want, I'll let you think about it for a moment. Could I go and get you another drink?" Zachary asked, trying to gauge from her expression what she was thinking.

"Okay. I'll let you get me another drink, but would you please just get me a glass of water with lemon? I think that I have had all the punch I need for one night. I'll have an answer for you by the time you get back. Thank you, Zachary," Madison replied and handed him her glass.

She watched as he turned his back to her and walked inside. The light hit him a bit, and she noticed he had a nice body; he obviously took care of himself. As she looked closer, she thought that he was about six five or so, and she could see that he did have a little ponytail, just like the one she had seen on him the first time she laid eyes on him in that wrecker. Now she knew that this was the man for her. Only, she didn't know what she was going to say to him when he came back.

She wanted to work for him, but in the back of her mind she kept thinking of the "no mixing business with pleasure" mantra she always told herself. But she really wanted to see him again. Could she live with just working for him and nothing else? Could she see him everyday and not get attached and want more? Would she even like him if she started spending time with him? Was he just a wrecker driver, or something more? Was he the owner? Partner? She didn't know, but had to make a decision quick. She wanted to see him no matter what the outcome. Madison sat on the bench and thought about what he'd asked her. Did she have time to go and do this job herself? Could she find the time? He was beautiful, and she wanted to, but by the same token, she hadn't thought about doing something so spur of the moment in a long time. She actually smiled when she thought of having her hands in a project, her hands alone.

She glanced at her watch and noticed that a full seven minutes had passed. She took in a deep breath and exhaled slowly, trying to make up her mind. Her senses kicked into overdrive, and she heard footsteps approaching her. She turned and saw Zachary coming toward her.

"Sorry it took me a long time. The line was long, and one of the clients I know stopped me and started chatting." Zachary paused and handed Madison her water. She was so exquisite.

"Thank you. It's all right. I understand about being stopped by clients. Anyhow, it gave me a chance to think about my decision." Madison paused, wondering what type of client would be here who would stop and talk to a wrecker driver. She knew what her heart was saying and knew what her answer was going to be, but she couldn't believe she was actually going to accept his proposal to be his personal designer.

"Zachary, before I give you my decision, I must warn you that I am not cheap. I—" Madison stopped and then started to say something when Zachary interrupted her.

"Madison, money isn't a problem. If it would make you feel better, I'll write you a check now for five thousand dollars, and there's more once you agree and we start picking out designs and colors."

Zachary couldn't stop smiling. Was she actually going to do this project herself? Was she going to be in his house? He just wanted her around; this was his soul mate, he just knew it. She probably thought that there was no way he could afford her company, but the truth of the matter was that he had quite a bit of money and could always get more.

Madison thought she was dreaming. She blinked her eyes and realized that Zachary Mann was true and standing before her, offering her five thousand dollars just to prove that he did have the money to hire her services.

"Okay, Zachary. I'll come to your home and see what I can do. But you don't have to give me any money at this point." Madison reached into her purse and withdrew a small piece of paper. "I'll give you my phone number, both home and office, and you can call me to set a time for your consultation."

Madison wrote down her numbers and handed the paper to Zachary. Zachary folded the little piece of paper and placed it in his shirt pocket.

"Thank you, Madison. I promise that you won't regret your decision. You'll even enjoy this project," Zachary said, thinking that hopefully by the time things got going on his home, things between them would be going as well. Zachary was ready to handle this project. More than anything, he was ready for Madison Trent in his life now and, if all went well, forever.

"Madison? Madison? Hello? Earth to Madison! Madison, where are you?" Abigail asked. She had came over to hang out with Madison and find out how the conference and dinner went, but so far Madison seemed like she was a million miles away.

"Oh, sorry, Abigail. I don't know what has gotten into me," Madison said, although she knew exactly what had gotten into her, and his name was Zachary Mann. Madison still couldn't believe that she had finally met him and that he had asked her to come and work for him. This was too good to be true. Madison had set up an appointment to meet Zachary at his house on Thursday of this week, but she still had four days before that was going to happen. She couldn't get over the fact that she had agreed to meet him; it was so unlike her.

Abigail looked at her friend and handed her another glass of Dr. Pepper.

"I want to know what's going on. Have you talked to Luke?" Abigail asked. She had curled up on the couch and was waiting for an answer. The two women hadplanned to go out and do some shopping, and maybe even meet up with Mark and Luke. When Abigail arrived, it began to rain, so the two decided to hang out and visit for a while. They ordered pizza, popped popcorn, and were sitting in Madison's spacious living room.

"No, I haven't talked to Luke. I need to call him, but I've just been so busy. We thought about getting together today with you guys, but I haven't talked to him yet. I just don't know about him. I mean, the conference and dinner just ended last night. Luke is really nice, Abigail, but please don't expect too much out of this. I mean, we've only had a couple of dates," Madison said while pausing to look at her best friend. She knew that Abigail was going to ask questions, and she was trying to figure out how she would answer.

"Okay, Madison. I'm not buying any of this. I think that there is something else going on, and I want to know what it is. Are you dating someone else? Or better yet, you're not pregnant, are you? You haven't even slept with Luke, or have you?" Abigail looked down at Madison's tummy nervously.

"No, I'm not dating anyone else, and no, I'm not pregnant. Are you nuts? Nothing is going on," Madison stated, hoping that Abigail would give up.

"Spill it, Madison. Where have you been all afternoon? I mean, you've talked and all, but I get a feeling that you're leaving something out. You can tell me; I'm your best friend. I promise that I won't make fun of you. And if you're in any type of trouble, we can get through it together," Abigail replied, getting serious and wondering if something was wrong with Madison.

"Nothing's really going on. I've decided that I'm

going to do a hands-on job, and I'm just thinking about all of that. I'm just trying to figure out how I'm going to juggle everything," Madison answered, hoping that Abigail would stop there and not pry anymore. Madison wasn't ready to tell anyone about Zachary Mann. She wanted to keep this a secret. She thought that this was too good to be true, and she didn't want to expose it and lose it all.

"Okay," Abigail began, "I still think that something is going on, but for whatever reason, you're not telling me. I guess that I'll just have to wait."

For the rest of the afternoon, Abigail and Madison flipped through magazines and the channels on the TV. The rain outside continued to drizzle down at a fast beat. It usually was soothing for Madison but not today. She couldn't wait until Thursday, when she would get to see Zachary again. She knew that she would have to get her emotions in line and be 100 percent professional. *Zachary probably has a serious love interest at the moment anyhow,* she thought and sighed.

Before Madison knew it, Thursday had arrived. All morning she had been in staff meetings and client meetings, so before she looked at her watch, it read two o'clock. Madison was anticipating her visit to Zachary's house. He had given her the address, and she knew the area but couldn't pick out what street he lived on. She was really anxious to go to his house, but worried at the same time that she would discover he was involved, or worse—married. "Stop it," she told herself.

She never mixed business with pleasure, so why was she starting to now? Besides, he already told her that he wasn't married.

"Madison?" Megan was at the door, holding some paperwork.

"Hey, Mom. Come on in. I was just taking a breather from all the meetings this morning. I think we may have a new client. It's to design a series of apartments. Apparently these apartments are going to be furnished and ready to move into. They are supposed to call us back by the end of next week with their decision." Madison smiled. She loved when people wanted her company, and it made her feel good.

"That's great, honey. I know whatever designs you gave them were our best. I was going to drop off these papers for you to sign. The one on the top is a contract for one of the projects that one of the staff members is working on. I think that you'll be pleased with what they are willing to pay you." Megan paused, letting Madison read over the contract.

"Wow, that's great," Madison said while signing her name. The rest were just correspondence from other clients and letters that Madison had sent out to them. Madison glanced down at her watch, and now it read three o'clock.

"I've got to get ready to go," Madison told her mom as she started getting her briefcase loaded with supplies that she would need for Zachary's house.

"Where are you going?" Megan asked.

"Oh, I forgot to tell you. I don't want you to get bent out of shape over this. I want to do this, and no one made me do it. I'm going to take on a job myself and do it myself. I haven't personally handled a job in such a long time, and now is the time for me to do it." Madison paused, looking at her mother.

"So let me get this straight. On top of everything else that Trent Design has going on right now, you are going to take on another client, and you're going to do this one hands-on?" Megan stopped and looked at her daughter. She knew that once Madison had set her mind to something there was little to nothing she could do.

"Yes, that's correct. I'm going to be handling this client after hours and on weekends. The client isn't in a big hurry, and they don't mind if it is on the back burner," Madison answered. She didn't want her mother to know that the client was a man. She would have blown the situation way out of the water.

"Okay, well, have fun, but just remember to get rest and not stress out," Megan said while getting up and heading out of the office.

Madison continued to pack her briefcase with everything she thought she might need. She wanted to be sure. She got the sample books and set them beside her briefcase so that she wouldn't forget them. Madison then buzzed her secretary and told her that she was going to meet with a client and that all calls should be filtered through Megan. At exactly three thirty, she was headed toward her SUV. She placed the sample books and her briefcase in the backseat, and off she headed toward Zachary Mann's home.

* * *

Zachary had not been this excited in a long time. He looked down at his watch and noticed that it was only 2:30 p.m., he was supposed to meet Madison Trent at his house at four sharp, and he did not want to be late. But he still had another hour before he had to leave. He started on some paperwork to try to distract him from thinking of Madison. He could not wait for her to see his home and for him to see her. Zachary was certain that she was the woman of his dreams.

* * *

Madison arrived about ten minutes early to Zachary's house. She noticed that he wasn't home, so she decided that she would look around and see if she got any ideas from what she could see on the outside. She got out of her SUV and started toward the backyard. Just as she reached the gate, she heard a bark and froze. She had not expected to find a dog back there. She peeked over the fence and noticed that it was a bulldog. *He looks cute enough,* she thought. She kneeled down, whistled at the dog, and over he ran, with slobber hanging out of his mouth. Madison decided that he was friendly and reached down to pet him. Just as soon as she did so, she felt a hand on her shoulder. Madison made a slight yell and turned on her heels to see who was behind her, knowing full who it was. At the same time, the dog was barking. Now she knew why the dog was coming over to the fence; Zachary was standing behind her; for how long, she didn't know.

"How long have you been standing there?" Madison asked.

"Oh, long enough to see that you almost met my dog," Zachary responded, ready for a little teasing session.

"Sorry. I didn't mean to be snooping. I just arrived about ten minutes ago and thought I would take a look around. I didn't expect you to have a dog. He's cute. Does he have a name?" Madison asked, thinking that Zachary was so handsome.

"His name is Spanky, and he is friendly. Aren't you, Spanky?" Zachary said, now turning his attention to his dog and leaning over to pet him.

"Shall we get started?" Zachary asked.

"Sure. Lead the way," Madison answered.

Zachary led Madison to the front of the house, where she stopped to get her briefcase and samples out of her SUV and followed Zachary into the house. The minute she stepped inside, she had a lot of ideas. There was so much that could be done, and she was truly excited she had taken on this job. Actually, she was excited to find out more about this man standing about three feet away from her.

"Welcome to my home. Please make yourself comfortable. Would you like a glass of tea or perhaps coffee?" Zachary asked while leading her into the dining area and motioning her to place all of her samples on the table.

"Tea would be nice, thank you," Madison replied as she looked around the rooms.

"Here you are," Zachary said while he handed Madison her glass of tea.

"Thank you. This house is beautiful. I can't wait to get started. What do you have in mind? Have you decided which room that you want me to redecorate?" Madison asked, trying to keep her mind from shifting from business to the man standing beside her. She glanced at him and noticed that he looked a little tired maybe, but nevertheless, beautiful.

"Well, I really haven't decided which room. Why don't I show you around and you can help me pick which one needs the most work. Follow me," Zachary said and started leading her into the living room.

For the next hour, they went from room to room, where Zachary gave a slight idea or suggestion or talked about what a particular room meant to him. Madison was in awe of all of the stuff he had. With her experience decorating, most bachelors had shot glasses lining a wall, or mismatched pictures or furniture. But not Zachary, his house was beyond belief. All the pictures matched and actually went with the room really well. The furniture was big but looked comfortable. He had colors of browns and tans with just a hint of red. She already liked it, and wondered what he wanted her to do different. When they finally reached the master bedroom, Madison could feel the butterflies starting up again. *What is wrong with me,* she thought?

"This is the master bedroom and bath. I really picked this house because of this room. It is big and spacious, and I like the open feeling," Zachary said, not knowing why he was rambling.

"This room is wonderful. There is so much that you can do with a room this size," Madison responded while looking around to see if anything suggested a woman. All she saw on the dresser were a couple bottles of cologne and a watch, nothing at all suspicious.

They walked to the other rooms while Madison took notes and tried to decide which room they should attack first. She was excited. She hadn't felt like this in a while and didn't want this feeling to end; and then her cell phone rang. Only a few people knew her number, so she figured that it must be the office or her mom or even possibly Abigail.

"Excuse me one minute," Madison said while taking her phone off her belt and turning away to answer.

"This is Madison Trent," Madison said in her best business voice, even though she knew that she was somewhat nervous.

"Hello, sweetheart. You're a hard woman to get a hold of." Luke's voice rang into her ear.

"Hi, how have you been?" Madison didn't know what to say. She had Luke on the line, and the man that drove her crazy was in front of her. She held up her finger to suggest giving her just a couple of minutes. Zachary smiled and headed into the kitchen.

"I'm fine but missing you. I was wondering if you wanted to get together tonight for dinner. I haven't seen you and thought it was about time for another date. What do you say?" Luke asked. He had sat in his office for the last hour debating whether he should call her or not. He knew that she was a busy woman, but he really liked her, and he wanted to pursue taking their relationship to the next level. He didn't really want to wait; he just wanted her.

"Oh, I don't know. I've been extremely busy. By the way, how did you get this number? I don't remember giving it to you," Madison asked.

"I called your office and talked to your mom. She gave it to me. And I must say that she is quite friendly. So how about dinner? I won't take no for an answer. I'll pick you up at your house at seven o'clock sharp. So what do you say, you have to eat you know," Luke said, pausing. Noticing that she wasn't saying no, he took it upon himself to assume she'd go. "Okay then, it's settled. I'll see you at seven. Bye for now," Luke said, ending the call.

Madison couldn't believe her ears. Luke wanted to be at her house in two hours. What was she going to do? How did she ever agree to this dinner? *Oh right*, she thought, *I didn't agree to it.*

"Something wrong?" Zachary's voice interrupted her thoughts.

"Nothing major, just the office calling," Madison lied smoothly. "Okay, let's continue this tour and discuss what you want to accomplish in your redecorating." Madison paused and then headed into the kitchen, where she sat down and started going through her briefcase.

"Well, I haven't really made up my mind on any one thing. I would like your opinion. After all, you are the professional." Zachary stated. *Wow, she is so beautiful,* he thought. He had to keep himself under control.

Over the next thirty minutes, Madison and Zachary talked about color schemes and if Zachary knew what type of design or statement he was wanting in the room that he chose. He thought that maybe Madison was worried about the money, but she didn't know that he could afford whatever he really wanted. But he knew that she was probably trying to figure out just how much she could spend on his house. He kind of liked leaving her in the dark, but knew that he would have to be honest and give her an amount soon enough.

"Madison, would you like to stay for dinner? I laid out some steaks. I would love your company, and we could finish our discussion," Zachary asked, knowing full well that she would probably say no.

"I would love to, but I have another obligation tonight, which, as a matter of fact, I need to get going," Madison answered. She had an hour and a half to get home and get herself dressed for dinner with Luke. She liked Luke, but she wasn't ready for a relationship that was pushy, and she didn't appreciate Luke just telling her that he was going to pick her up at a particular time.

"Okay, I understand. I guess that Spanky will just get a great dinner tonight. I wish you could stay, but I get it. But I would like to take you to dinner one night. Do I need to call your secretary and set up a time?" Zachary said, halfway teasing and the other half serious.

"No, I'll tell you what. Why don't we have lunch on Monday, and then we can go and look at some fabric? That way, you will have the week to decide what room you would like me to start on," Madison said and smiled. She would have loved to stay, but she knew that if she didn't meet Luke, she would never hear the end of it.

"Okay, I guess that I'll have to settle for that," Zachary replied, wondering if what he felt was just one sided. "Thank you so much for coming over and agreeing to take on this project. I know you're a busy woman," Zachary said, as he walked her to the door.

"You're welcome. I'll call you on Monday and let you know where to meet me. Have a good evening," Madison responded as she carried her samples and briefcase out to the SUV. She couldn't believe that she was actually going to do this. He was so handsome, and she just knew that he must have a girlfriend. She wanted to find out more, but for now she was going to have to put that to the side and get through this date with Luke.

* * *

While driving home, Madison was thinking, and thinking way too much. She liked Luke and thought that he was a great guy, but he didn't make her heart pitter-patter and her knees get weak. She wondered if she was being too hard on him. Maybe she should give him a chance. After all, they had only been out a handful of times. *Okay,* she thought, *I'm going to have fun and try not to think about the man that does make my heart pitter-patter and my knees weak.*

* * *

At exactly seven o'clock, the doorbell rang, and there stood Luke with a bouquet of flowers.

"These are for you, and I must say that you look absolutely, beautifully dangerous in that outfit," Luke said. She looked good enough to eat right there, but he would wait until later and see where the night ended. He hoped in his house, in his bed.

"Thank you. They're beautiful," Madison said while inviting Luke inside her house. He did look good, but not as good as … *Oh, stop it,* she told herself. *Give him a chance.*

"Would you like a drink before we headed out to dinner?" Madison asked.

"Actually, no. I made us reservations at the new restaurant in upper Houston. We need to get going, but I'll take a rain check on that drink." He helped Madison into her shawl as they headed out.

"I hope that you're hungry," Luke said.

"Yes, I am. I have to say, Luke, that I'm sorry I've been ignoring you lately," Madison responded, trying hard to give him a chance.

"I accept your apology. Now, let's have a great time," Luke answered as he opened the door for Madison to get in.

It was a thirty-minute drive, but tonight, for some reason, it felt much longer to Madison. The drive was somewhat silent, and she thought that Luke felt some type of tension as well. She was trying to overcome the tension and make conversation, even though her mind was definitely not on Luke. They had talked but not about anything in particular, just really the basic conversations—the weather, work stuff, and friends. Finally, Luke got restless and turned down the radio, which was already at a low volume.

"Is there something on your mind that you would like to tell me about?" Luke asked.

"No, Luke, don't be silly. I'm just enjoying the ride and the company. It's been a long week," Madison answered.

"Well, I would like to talk to you about something that is very important to me. I was going to wait until dinner, but maybe I should just get it over with so we can enjoy the rest of the evening," Luke said, wondering what he was going to say and how Madison would respond.

"Sure, Luke. What's on your mind?" Madison asked, wondering what was going on.

"Well—" Luke began, but Madison's cell phone rang.

"I'm so sorry, Luke. Just give me a minute." Madison reached in her purse for her cell phone, wondering who was calling her.

"Hello?" Madison said.

"Hi, Madison." *Oh no,* she thought, *not the voice.* The voice only belonged to one man, and that one man made her whole life spin upside down.

"Hello to yourself. What's up?" Madison asked, trying to act as though nothing was going on and that she wasn't sitting in a vehicle with another man.

"I was just going to tell you that you left some paperwork over here. I glanced at the papers and found your cell phone number. I wanted to tell you immediately, in case the papers are important." Zachary paused, so happy that he called her, and she actually sounded happy to talk to him.

"Oh, I didn't realize that I had left any work. Thank you for calling me about it. I will pick it up tomorrow about ten, if that is okay with you," Madison said, trying to think of exactly what was left over at Zachary's house.

"Tomorrow morning is perfect. Tell you what, I'll have breakfast ready when you get here. I'll see you later then," Zachary said and hung up the phone before Madison would give an excuse of any kind.

"Bye," Madison said into her cell phone; knowing Zachary had already hung up. She couldn't believe her ears. Zachary Mann was going to make her breakfast in the morning. Wow!

"Who was that?" Luke asked, wanting to know if it was a man or not.

"Oh, just a client," Madison replied. "I forgot some paperwork over at their house, so I'll pick it up in the morning," Madison finished. "So, what were you saying earlier?"

"Well, it will wait until dinner now. We're here," Luke said while he pulled up his truck to the valet parking.

When Madison got out of the truck, Luke was right there waiting and reached for her hand. It caught her off guard. *What was into Luke tonight?* Granted, he was gorgeous and smart and had money, but something was missing. Maybe Luke realized it too and was going to tell her tonight that they shouldn't see each other anymore. Luke led her into the restaurant, and they were immediately seated.

"I hope that you like this place," Luke said.

"Wow, Luke. This place is really beautiful. Have you been here before?" Madison asked while looking around at all of the spectacular lighting and pictures.

"I've been here a couple of times before and remember the food to be excellent. What would you like to drink?" Luke asked while nodding toward one of the waiters, who promptly came over and greeted Luke.

"Welcome Mr. Davidson. I haven't seen you in here lately. How's business?" the waiter asked.

"Oh, business is good. Thanks for asking. I think that we would like to start off with a couple of iced teas," Luke said.

"Yes, sir. I'll be right back," the waiter said and then headed off to the kitchen.

"I think that you have been here more than a couple of times for him to know your name," Madison said, wondering if he came here all the time.

"Okay, I'll tell you, but just because I don't want you to think that I bring all my dates here. I'm part owner in this restaurant. I don't tell many people. Mark knows, and that is probably it. It's no big deal. So let's enjoy tonight and relax." Madison was just going to comment on his spacious and romantic restaurant when the waiter appeared with their drinks. Madison assumed it was the house ice tea, as the liquid looked a bit of a different color.

"Here's to tonight," Luke said while handing Madison her glass.

"Tonight," Madison echoed and tapped her glass to his.

The atmosphere at dinner was romantic and elegant. Madison was trying really hard to give Luke a chance, but deep down she wondered what Zachary was doing tonight. Did he really give his dog, Spanky, a steak, or did he call someone else over to eat her steak? The dinner was absolutely delicious, and by the time that dessert came out, Madison was laughing and actually enjoying herself in Luke's company.

They talked about Abigail and Mark. They agreed that the two of them made a perfect pair.

"Do you ever think they will get married?" Madison asked.

"I'm not really sure. I know that Mark would love to get married one day, but he might be a little scared to ask the question. I think that he is scared of the answer being no," Luke responded.

Madison laughed. "Believe me, if Mark asked Abigail to marry him, I could almost guarantee you that she would say yes. He's all that she talks about; they're together every minute of every waking day. She adores him, and I think that he adores her back. Speaking of them, I really need to give Abigail a call. I know that she had a huge court trial starting, and like me, when she gets busy, the whole world almost disappears." Madison stopped and took a bite of the mouth-watering cheesecake. It was awesome.

"Madison, I want you to know that I've really enjoyed this evening." Luke paused, letting that sink in and wondering how he was going to tell her what he had wanted to tell her from the moment he met her.

"I have enjoyed this evening as well. Thank you for asking me to dinner," Madison said. Suddenly, the pit of her stomach started feeling a weird sensation. Maybe something was in the tea, but this seemed a little different, maybe like nerves. What was going on with her?

"Madison," Luke started and reached for her hand. "I know that we've only been on a handful of dates and phone calls, but I really enjoy your company, and I really like you. I would like to make a suggestion. I would like us to commit to each other and only each other so that we can take the step to the next level of our relationship. I knew that we would make an awesome team from the moment I met you at the Pelican Bar. I could really see myself falling in love with you. I want to have that chance. I know that all of this is sudden, and I'll give you time to think it over, but I really am just bubbling over with feelings for you, and I want an opportunity to find those feelings and act on them."

Madison's heart just stopped, and she was suddenly very uncomfortable. What was Luke talking about? Did he just say that he could fall in love with her? She didn't know how to respond. She would definitely have to think this over. She liked Luke, and they did have a good time when they were together; but Madison didn't ever think of moving their relationship to the next level, like Luke wanted to do. Was he crazy? Or was she crazy for not jumping on the offer to make a commitment?

"Madison, say something. I know that this is a lot to take in all at once," Luke said, still holding her hand all this time.

"Luke, I don't know what to say," Madison began. "I'll definitely have to think this over. I don't know if I'm ready for a commitment, and, oh, I just don't know. There are a lot of things that we should know about each other before we make a commitment; like what we like and dislike, if you go to church, if you want kids, all of that," Madison finished and pulled her hand out of Luke's and placed it in her lap.

"Madison, take all the time you need, but just remember," Luke began and then lowered his voice so that only she could hear him, "I'm a great guy with a lot to offer any woman, so don't wait to long, or it might be too late." Luke stood up, left a large tip, and smiled at Madison.

Madison stood, still in amazement that Luke said something so conceited and gutsy. Madison didn't know how to respond. It was as if she were just in a daze. She decided to just let things go and to think all of this out over a nice, long, bath alone. She knew that Luke wouldn't be too happy with her decision to be alone tonight, but he would have to deal with it. Madison wanted a Christian man, someone she could grow old with, and she didn't think that Luke was that person. She would go home and say a prayer for guidance on what she was supposed to do. But she was still in shock over what Luke had just told her.

Luke led her out to the waiting truck, and he opened her door for her. Madison climbed in and sat there, wondering what she was going to say and or do. Luke got in the truck, placed it in gear, and off they started toward home.

About ten minutes passed before Luke said anything.

Madison had not responded the way in which Luke had thought she would. They had had such a great time on the boat. Something was different about Madison lately, and he wanted to know what it was. Luke was not a very patient man. Usually he got what he wanted when he wanted it, and Madison would be no different, or so he thought.

"Madison, would you like to come over for a night-cap?" Luke asked.

"Luke, I appreciate the offer, but I think that I just need to go home. I have a lot to think over, and I don't want to hurt your feelings. Please don't take it personally, but I think it's better if I go home alone tonight," Madison said and then paused to look at Luke. He was undeniably gorgeous, and most women would jump at the chance to be with him. But for Madison, there was something missing. Something that she had to have in a relationship. There was another man that did make Madison feel all giddy with butterflies in the pit of her stomach.

"Okay, I respect your decision. I'll take you home

tonight," Luke answered. He was trying not to sound upset, but he didn't know if it worked. He was angry; he knew that a lot of women would love to have him, and he didn't know why Madison Trent didn't. He could call up any of his old girlfriends, and any of them would jump at the opportunity to have a relationship with him. But most of them bored him, and he simply dismissed them.

Luke pulled up in the driveway and sat there, not knowing what to say. He reminded himself that he was a gentleman and got out of the truck and went to help Madison out.

"Thank you for dinner, Luke. I'll think about our relationship, and I'll let you know once I've made a decision. I know that there are probably a lot of women who would love to have you, but the comment that you made in the restaurant wasn't necessary. I don't do well with threats, and I don't like to feel pressured to make a decision. I respect you for telling me how you feel. Now I ask that you respect me and let me think this through," Madison said. She turned to head toward the front door, but Luke caught her arm and pulled her back toward him.

"I'll give you some time to think, but I recommend you don't wait too long. Thank you for going to dinner with me. I'll call your office at the end of the week, and I'll be waiting for your answer," Luke replied. He didn't know what was going on. He always had women coming on to him all the time and now this one didn't really want to continue the relationship. He just didn't get that. Why? What was wrong with her? He was successful, handsome, and had it all. Who wouldn't want to be with him?

* * *

Madison watched as he pulled out of the driveway and then shut the front door. What was she going to do? Was she going to give Luke a commitment and a chance, or what? What about Zachary? She really didn't know anything about Zachary, didn't know if he had a girlfriend or if he even liked her. She would have to weigh her chances and what she wanted in life. She knew that she wanted a long-term relationship with a good man; someone with morals, someone who would have faith like she did, and someone who would make her heart skip a beat from just listening to his voice. Madison went into the bathroom, turned on the faucets, and let the steam heat up her bathroom. Madison undressed and slid into the warm water and let the tub continue to fill up.

Madison had a very hard decision to make but not as hard as she thought. She liked Luke but felt as though her heart was somewhere else. Was she crazy for stepping out in faith for Zachary? Should she go with Luke—the man she knew liked her and had a lot to offer? Or did she take a chance on Zachary, hoping he wasn't seeing someone, that he would like her, and that she would like him once she got to know him. Zachary definitely did make her knees weak and her heart stop when she looked at him. What type of man did she want to spend the rest of her life with? Madison closed her eyes and relaxed, knowing that her heart was telling her one thing, but her mind was trying to open the door to be fair to each man.

* * *

Madison tossed and turned for most of the night. She woke up and glanced at the clock, and it read only 4:30 A.M. She couldn't sleep; she didn't know what was keeping her up, the demands from Luke or the thought of Zachary. She crawled out of bed and decided that she would get a drink, maybe take something to help her sleep, and take care of the dull headache that was trying to reach the surface.

She walked through her house and thought how quiet it was. *Wow,* she thought to herself. She had never thought her house was quiet and had always enjoyed her haven. She reached the kitchen and noticed that her phone was blinking from a missed call. She picked it up and looked to see who would have called her in the middle of the night. She pushed the retrieve button, and Luke's name and number popped up. She noticed that the time he called was 3:00 a.m. What was he still doing up, and what in the world was he doing calling her that late? Things like that really bothered Madison. She liked to be in control, and with Luke, he wanted the control. She got a glass of water and a Motrin, still amazed at what her life had become. A month ago, she didn't have anyone, and now she had Luke, who wanted more than she thought she could offer. Then there was Zachary, her mystery man. Madison got back into bed and pulled the covers up to her head.

Madison had just fallen back into a deep sleep when her alarm went off. She rolled over and noticed that she had set her alarm for eight and wondered why she had when she didn't have to go to work or anything. She lay her head back on her pillow and then shot straight up in bed. "Oh my goodness," she said, realizing that she was supposed to be at Zachary's at ten to pick up her work, and he was going to cook her breakfast. Madison got out of bed and went into the bathroom. As she passed the mirror, she paused and noticed that her eyes were a bit puffy and dark. "Great, just what I needed," she muttered as she started the shower.

Zachary was in an excellent mood this morning. He woke up at six, which was a bit early for him. But he knew that today might be the beginning of something big, and something that he definitely wanted. He walked into the kitchen and noticed that Spanky was sitting by his bowls. "Hungry, big guy?" Zachary asked while he patted Spanky's head and poured him some food. It was nice to have a pet. You always knew that they loved you and depended on you. Zachary's thoughts turned to Madison. He hadn't been in a serious relationship in a long time, and he was ready to settle down. Maxine was always telling him it was time to find his soul mate, get married, and have a couple of kids to fill this big house. Thinking of Maxine, he picked up the phone and called her. Maxine was very predictable. She was always up by 6:15, enjoying a cup of coffee and reading the paper before she came to work. She always filled everyone in on the current events of what was going on in the world.

"Hi, Max. It's me," Zachary said when he heard her pick up the phone.

"Good morning, Zachary. What are you doing up so early? What gives?" Maxine asked curiously.

"Well, I'm cooking breakfast this morning and wondered what I should cook," Zachary asked. He was a good cook. Years of being a bachelor at least taught him how to cook, and the rest Maxine had helped him with.

"Who are you cooking breakfast for, and did you have an overnight guest? You know how I feel about you acting irresponsible, Zach," Maxine stated. She thought of Zachary as her own son and treated him as such.

"No, I didn't have an overnight guest. I'll have to tell you all about it later. Would you please help me decide on what I should cook?" Zachary said, thankful that he had someone in his life that kept his best interests at heart.

"Well, it sounds like you don't know this person very well. I would cook something traditional like pancakes, bacon, and eggs. I would offer coffee and juice. If you have any flowers around, you might set them on the table if you want something cheery," Maxine responded, wondering why Zachary was so nervous about breakfast. She thought that maybe Zachary had finally met his match and this could be his special someone. "Enjoy your breakfast, and I'll see you at the office," Maxine said and hung up the phone.

That was weird, Zachary thought. Maxine had let the conversation go and did not pick at him for details. That in itself was a miracle. But she did have a good idea about the flowers. He glanced at the clock, and it was only seven. He had plenty of time. He pulled out the phone book and looked up his buddy who just happened to own a flower shop. He placed the order for a mixed bouquet, colorful and big, and it was supposed to be over by nine. *Well, at least I have that done,* he thought and sat down at the table to drink a cup of coffee while he waited for the clock to slowly move toward ten.

Madison was never late, but this morning in particular she felt like she was going to be. She didn't know what to wear. She didn't even think that she could eat in front of this magnificently made man. She glanced at her watch and noticed that it was already nine. *Good,* she thought as she picked up her phone and dialed the office.

"Good morning, Trent Design," Sandi stated.

"Good morning, Sandi," Madison replied. "Would you place me through to Megan?"

"Sure thing, Ms. Trent," Sandi answered and patched her through. "Good morning, Madison," Megan answered.

"Good morning, Mom. Listen, I have a breakfast appointment with a client, so I probably won't be in until about noon. I don't have anything pending, but if anything pops up, you can take care of it for me. I'll have my phone on if you need me," Madison said coolly. She didn't want her mom to notice the slight hitch in her voice. After all, Madison didn't want to answer a million questions that she wasn't ready for yet.

"Okay, sweetheart. I'll take care of everything for you. See you when you get in," Megan responded.

Madison hung up the phone and thought that went better than what she expected. She finished curling her hair and applying her makeup; she wanted to look flawless. *I'm ready,* she thought as she reached for her purse and cell phone and then once again remembered that Luke had called her in the middle of the night last night. *Okay, I'll deal with that today as well, but first I'm going to have breakfast with the man of my dreams.* She locked her front door and jumped into her SUV. She was in an amazing mood.

Fifteen minutes later, Madison pulled up into Zachary's driveway and got out of her SUV. She was excited and nervous. "You're fine," she told herself and walked up confidently to the front door and rang the doorbell. Once the door opened, she realized that her life was never going to be the same. Madison took a deep breath and said a silent prayer. *Lord, lead me. If this mystery man is supposed to be in my life, please give me a sign. Amen.*

Zachary heard Madison pull up. *Right on time,* he thought and double-checked to make sure that everything was perfect. The flowers were an excellent touch. The doorbell rang. He paused, took a deep breath, and went to the door. On the other side of that door was the woman that he had been waiting his whole life for.

"Good morning. Hope you brought your appetite," Zachary said while he escorted Madison inside.

"Good morning to you, and yes, I brought my appetite," Madison responded, hoping that the food stayed down. Her nerves were in high gear. Zachary looked so beautiful. She could feel the butterflies invading her whole stomach. She quickly swallowed and hoped that Zachary didn't catch the look that she sent him.

Zachary led the way into the kitchen and pulled out her chair. He couldn't believe that Madison was in his home and that it felt so right. She sat down in the chair, and he got a whiff of a soft fragrance that drove him wild. *What is wrong with me?* Zachary thought. He felt his cheeks flush and tried to settle his thoughts.

"Would you like coffee or juice?" Zachary asked, trying to shift his thoughts to something boring and to get this woman out of his mind.

"Coffee would be great. I've tried to quit drinking coffee first thing in the mornings, but it's just hard. I feel like I need that burst of energy. Wow, I haven't played hooky from work in forever. This is nice." *Where did that come from?* Madison wondered. *That sounded so dorky.* What was Zachary thinking of her now? She thought she sounded like a rambling teenager. *What should we talk about,* Madison thought, *to get my mind off him and onto something of an even playing field?*

"So, have you decided what you would like me to do for your house and when you would like me to start?" Madison asked Zachary as she got out her notebook and pen.

"I thought that maybe you could start on the living room. Bacon or sausage?" Zachary asked.

"Bacon. What would you like to accomplish in your living room?" Madison asked while she sipped her coffee.

"I would like to bring a bit of color to the room but also to make it inviting and cozy. I enjoy my space, and I want anyone who walked into the house to enjoy it too," Zachary replied, wondering what Madison had going on in her head. Man, it was driving him insane.

"Okay, that gives me some ideas," Madison said while Zachary set down a plate of pancakes, bacon, and eggs. "This looks delicious," Madison said.

"Yeah, I think so too," Zachary stated, although he wasn't just talking about the food. "If you don't mind, I would like to say a prayer over our breakfast," Zachary asked as he bowed his head. Madison followed suit. "Dear Lord, thank you for this beautiful day. Thank you for the many blessings you've given us. Thank you for this food, and may it nourish us. Amen."

Wow, Madison thought, *did he really just pray?* This was incredible; she couldn't believe her luck in finding a man who was also a believer. For the next hour, they made small talk about work. They both had a lot in common; they found out they both were workaholics, attended church, but not as regularly as they should, and enjoyed the outdoors—especially fishing—when they had time. Before either one of them knew it, breakfast was over, and it was pushing noon.

"Well, the time has really flown by. Let me do the dishes. After all, you cooked," Madison said smoothly. "What would you like to do with the leftovers?" she questioned.

"Here, let me give them to Spanky. He always enjoys when he gets people food," Zachary replied while taking the plate and opening the back door.

Madison smiled and went to clearing off the table and started to put the dishes in the dishwasher. She caught herself humming and smiled. She realized that she liked this house, and she liked the man who owned this house. Now she just had to find out more about him.

Zachary turned around from feeding Spanky just in time to see Madison smile. *She looks so natural in my kitchen, in my house,* he thought. He wanted to get to know her better and to know if she was involved with anyone.

"Would you like to go to dinner with me tonight?" Zachary blurted before he had a chance to take it back or to even think about what he was asking.

"I'm sorry. What did you ask?" Madison said, putting down the dishtowel that she was holding. She thought that she just heard him ask her to dinner, and she wanted to make sure that was correct before she answered.

"Would you like to go to dinner?" Zachary answered while he came up to stand beside her. He could just smell the fragrance; it smelled a little floral with a hint of spice.

"I would love to, but I need to work late tonight and try to get some contracts completed," Madison said, kicking herself. She wanted to get to know this man, but she didn't want this man in particular to think that she didn't have anything better to do. Frankly, she didn't, but she didn't want Zachary to know about that, and plus, she really needed to take care of the Luke problem. "I'll see you Monday for lunch, though, and don't forget to have your thinking cap on because we'll be looking at fabric," Madison threw in quickly.

"Okay, I'll take a rain check for dinner. Let me get your paperwork that you left," Zachary said while walking into the living room to get Madison's samples. "What time do you want to meet on Monday?" Zachary asked.

"Why don't we meet at twelve thirty? Do you like Italian?" Madison questioned.

"Twelve thirty sounds good, and yes, I like just about anything," Zachary said.

"Let's meet at Carrabba's. You know where that is?" Madison asked.

"Yeah, that's a good place. I'll meet you there," Zachary replied. "Thank you for coming over to eat breakfast with me this morning. I don't eat breakfast very often since I'm usually at the office around eight or earlier," Zachary continued. Why he was talking so much, he didn't know.

"Thank you for inviting me. I really enjoyed our conversation, and I look forward to working for you," Madison stated coolly. She didn't want him to think she wanted anything else yet. She still had a lot of information to find out about him. Was he just a wrecker driver? Or was he the owner of the company? And most importantly, did he have a girlfriend? Or was there more to the picture? She tried to bring it up at breakfast, but somehow Zachary kept going around the question.

"See you Monday," Zachary replied as he walked Madison to the door.

"See you Monday," Madison stated and walked out the door.

Zachary watched her get into her SUV and then back out of the driveway. She was so beautiful. He wanted to know everything about her, and he wanted to know now. He chuckled and shut the door.

Madison arrived at her office a little after one. It was the latest she had ever arrived at work unless she was sick.

Madison turned and headed down the hall toward her office. She wanted to put her stuff down and then take a deep breath. Madison reached her office desk just in time to hear Megan walk in and sit down.

"Where have you been?" Megan said, now sounding more like a mom than an employee. "Oh, I had a breakfast appointment with a client, and it ran late. Remember? I called you this morning. How are things going this morning?" Madison questioned, trying not to sound like a lovesick schoolgirl.

"Oh, that's right. The appointment must have run long, it slipped my mind," Megan replied, feeling bad that she was questioning her daughter when she was working. "Nothing much going on today. I think everyone is trying to get their desks cleaned off before the weekend. Speaking of that, I have reviewed the contracts from the presentation with Noah and Dylan. They look really good, and the money looks good as well. Would you sign these so we can get them out in the mail by Monday?" Megan asked.

"Yeah, that was on my agenda for today. I don't have that much going on except for detail work. I need to order some fabric and supplies for Noah and Dylan. I'm excited about my project with them. I need to pick out my top decorators to go and make this happen. I would like you there as well, Mom. I have a new client, the one that I was telling you about that I'm going to be hands-on with, and I have to get ready for that too. Would you mind stepping in on the Noah and Dylan project? I'll make sure that you get a nice bonus," Madison said, smiling. She knew that her mom loved it when she wanted her to do something, and Megan knew that Madison would take care of her financially as well.

"I would love to step in. I think that Noah and Dylan will be a lot of fun to work with. And I know that you'll take care of me, so that shouldn't even cross your mind," Megan said, half emotionally. Madison helped her out so much. She had bought her a new car just last year, and everything was going so well. Her daughter had a lot to do with that.

"Okay then. It is settled," Madison stated.

"Okay, so tell me about this new client," Megan asked.

"Oh." Madison could feel her face get hot. She just

prayed that it didn't show through. "Well, I don't know too much yet. We are meeting on Monday to look at fabric and to see what he likes and doesn't like. I have realized one thing; I miss actually being hands on with a project. This will be fun," Madison answered, hoping that her mom would stop with all the questions.

"Okay, let me know if you need me to write up a contract or anything. Wow, I can't believe how big you are getting. I'm so proud of you," Megan responded, smiling.

"Thanks, Mom," Madison said, smiling.

Megan got up and left the office and left Madison to start to think about Zachary, but first she had to figure out what she was going to do about Luke. She glanced down and realized that it was already 2:15 P.M. *Where did the day go to?* She was pondering what she was going to do about Luke when Sandi interrupted her thoughts.

"Ms. Trent, you have a visitor. He said his name was Luke Davidson, and he is waiting in the conference room," Sandi said.

"Thank you, Sandi," Madison answered. *Speak of the devil,* she thought. She barely had any time to think about Zachary, much less what she was going to do about Luke. She stood up and went to her bathroom and glanced over herself. *I do look good,* she thought. She reapplied her lipstick and spritzed a little perfume. She didn't know what she was going to say to Luke or why he was there. She shrugged and walked out of her office.

Madison paused just outside of the doorway and peeked through the window. There was Luke standing by the window, looking out. He seemed to be deep in thought; he didn't even know that she was nearby.

Madison continued to observe him. He was dressed in a suit, and he did fill the suit out nicely. *He is really handsome,* she thought, looking at him from top to bottom. But he was still not enough to make her knees weak or to cause her to feel the butterflies. She sighed and walked into the room. Luke turned and smiled.

"Well, good afternoon, Ms. Trent. You look beautiful." Luke walked over and gave her a hug.

"Hello, Luke. What made you stop by today?" Madison asked, still wondering why he was here in her office. She then started to worry about how this would look to all the employees. She knew the rumors would be flying now. "I was in the neighborhood and was hungry, so I thought that I would see if you wanted to go to lunch. So what do you say?" Luke asked with that boyish grin.

"Oh, I'm sorry, Luke. I just came back from lunch," Madison answered. She was lying, but she didn't want to be alone with him. She knew that he was just going to put pressure on her to make a decision, and she didn't know exactly what she was going to say and how she was going to say it.

"Why do I get the feeling that you are trying to brush me off?" Luke asked.

"I'm not; I promise. I'm just busy today, trying to get contracts out." Madison paused and thought that she might as well get this over with this weekend or she was going to go crazy. "Why don't you come over tomorrow night for dinner, and we'll talk?" Madison asked Luke.

"Well, well, what an offer. How can I refuse?" Luke answered. He wanted some alone time with Madison, and this might just be the answer to his questions. "I would love to come over tomorrow night. What time?" Luke responded.

"Why don't you come over at seven?" Madison answered. Tonight would give her the time to think things over and to figure out what she was going to say to Luke. She wanted Zachary, but she didn't even know anything about him.

"Tomorrow it is," Luke replied and reached in and lightly planted a kiss on Madison's lips. "I hope that will tide you over until tomorrow night," Luke said and winked at her while he walked out of the conference room. Madison sat down in one of the oversized chairs and sighed. What was she going to do? Luke was successful and handsome. He would make anyone a good mate; but did she want him to be her mate? That was the question of the day. She would really need to say a prayer tonight to have courage to do what was right and to follow her heart. Luke's actions were a bit blatant, but she didn't know if she was just looking for something wrong with him. If she really liked him, would she still find him offensive? She just didn't really know. Her heart was telling her one thing, but she was somewhat scared to go with her heart. She still didn't know anything about Zachary, and here Luke was asking for more. What was she to do?

Madison readjusted her thoughts and walked back into her office and shut the door. She leaned against the door and frowned. She didn't want Luke to be the one coming over; she wanted Zachary. She thought Luke was a good guy, and he was a great catch, but did she want to catch him? She didn't know anything about

Zachary, and she needed to find out as much as she could before tomorrow night, and she would start her search right now. She sat down at her desk and thought that she would check the Internet. What would she look up? Just repossession companies or what? She didn't know much about that profession to know how to find one. She just guessed and punched in repossession companies in Houston. She watched the hourglass while it was thinking.

Meanwhile, Madison started daydreaming, thinking about how much fun it was in Zachary's house and how right it felt. Did she believe in love at first sight? She wasn't sure. She blinked when she glanced at her computer and saw Mann Co. Repossession Specialists. She paused. She wasn't sure if she wanted to know anything or not. Madison took a deep breath and double-clicked. To her amazement, the Web site for Mann Co. was impressive. She read the home page and noticed that the business had been around for thirty-plus years. *Wow,* she thought, *that's a long time.* She looked over to the right-hand side, and the headlines read, "Meet Mann Co.," "View Area of Coverage," "Contact Us." *What are the chances,* she thought. *I'm already here, might as well find out as much as possible.* She clicked on "Meet Mann Co.," and had to catch her breath. There in front of her was the most beautiful man she ever saw. Zachary Mann was staring back at her. *Well, well,* she thought, *he owns the company.* That was a surprise, not a shocking surprise but a pleasant one. He obviously wasn't the type to just sit in an office and push paperwork. He liked to get his hands dirty and be out in the field. Madison liked that type of man.

Okay, let's continue to look to see what else we can find. First of all, she wanted to know how the business was up and running for thirty-five years. Zachary would probably have been in grade school then. She continued to scroll down, and it gave a history of the company. The company was started in 1970 by Richard Mann. He had a son, Zachary, and had passed on the company to Zachary when he decided to retire. It seemed as though Zachary had been working this business ever since he could walk. *Interesting,* Madison thought.

She continued to browse the Web site and learned quite a bit. She learned that Zachary's repossession company was a member of ARA, which was an elite recovery association. Then the site went on to show the insured amount of coverage if a vehicle was damaged. There was a lot of information to read about repossessions. Madison had never given it much thought, but now it was just fascinating. She was clicking on every headline when her phone beeped, jarring her from her investigation.

"Yes?" Madison slipped accidentally.

"Ms. Trent, you have a delivery. Would you like me to bring it to your office?" Sandi asked.

"Just sign for it, and I'll be right up to get it," Madison stated, thinking that she had some more contracts to review or some samples of fabric that finally came in. Madison quickly clicked on favorites and put Mann Co. on her favorite list. She knew that she would want to look at him again or reread that he was the owner.

"Wow, here I thought that he was just a wrecker driver," Madison said out loud. She closed her Internet and got up and smiled. She really thought that she wanted to get to know Zachary more, and all this information just proved what she wanted. Now she had to find out if there was someone in his life, although the Web site didn't indicate there was a Mrs. Mann. She smiled again as she walked out of her office and up to the front, where her smile froze. There in front of her were a dozen yellow roses, the most beautiful that she had ever seen. She thought maybe there was a mistake and the deliveryman delivered the wrong thing.

"Sandi, what is this?" Madison asked, feeling the butterflies in her stomach starting to flutter.

"They are for you," Sandi said, smiling.

"Oh, thank you," Madison said while taking the flowers and turning straight back to her office. She received flowers occasionally from customers that loved her work, but they were always mixed flowers, not roses. And these roses had a certain type of personal touch to them. She walked into her office and sat the roses on her table, wondering who they were from. She took a deep breath and then reached for the card when her mom walked in.

"Oh, those are beautiful. Who are they from?" Megan asked curiously.

"I haven't opened up the card yet. Probably from a customer," Madison responded.

"Well, open it up," Megan said.

Madison took a deep breath and opened the card. She glared at the writing and felt disappointment set in.

The card read, "Here's to tomorrow night. Hope you enjoy them. Love, Luke."

"Well?" Megan asked. "Who are they from?" She

snatched the card from Madison's hand before she could do anything about it.

"Mom!" Madison said but didn't have the effort to try to defend herself because she knew that her mom would have plenty of questions.

"Who's Luke?" Megan asked. "What are you doing tomorrow night?" Megan asked again.

"Mom, don't get too excited. This isn't what you think. Why don't we sit down? I have a feeling this might take a while," Madison said and sunk down in her chair.

"Well, tell me about this Luke guy. How long have you been seeing him? Do you like him?" Megan was starting to drive Madison crazy, but she just wanted to know.

"Mom, okay. Don't take this the wrong way, but this is none of your business. I'll tell you this. Luke and I have gone out on a couple of dates, but I don't think that he is the one for me. He is a great guy, but I don't think that he is my great guy. Luke sent me these flowers because when we went out a couple of nights ago to dinner, he put some pressure on me to decide what I wanted from him. I don't want anything from him. I invited him over tomorrow night to tell him that, but I guess he might think that I have something else to tell him," Madison said and sighed. She felt exhausted. This morning she was on cloud nine, and now she felt like she just needed to crawl into bed.

"Are you sure that he couldn't be more to you, Madison?" Megan asked.

"Mom, I'm sure. He just doesn't do it for me. He's not the type of man that I need. He would be great to just have fun with but not to settle down with. That is what I need and what I am ready for. Please don't read more into this than what there is. I told you all of that because we are both adults, but if you're going to give me the third degree every time, then I won't tell you." Madison paused and then continued, "Mom, I'm sorry that I snapped at you. I just don't like someone, especially a man, to pressure me and to give me demands. I don't work like that," Madison finished and reached for her glass of water.

"I understand. I don't want you to do anything that you don't want. I'm proud of you for not settling and for not letting a man run your life. I know that you'll make a wise decision. But those roses are beautiful," Megan said while standing up and smelling the roses. "I will talk with you later. I'm going to leave a little early today. I love you. Have a good weekend," Megan said and blew Madison a kiss and then turned and walked out.

Madison was relieved that her mom had stopped asking so many questions. It wasn't as painful as she thought. She looked at her watch and realized that it was already 4:00 P.M. She looked at her desk and thought that she hadn't gotten anything done today, but she would just pack up and take the contracts and paperwork home with her. It had been a long week.

* * *

Zachary couldn't wait to see Madison again. She was smart, beautiful, and he wanted so much more from her. He knew deep down that they were supposed to be together. He believed that God puts everyone in your path for a reason, and the reason was so clear to him; he was supposed to be with Madison. He thought about asking her out for the weekend, but he didn't want to be pushy and overbearing, so he would wait until their luncheon on Monday to look at fabric. He really didn't know anything about fabric; he had just planned on letting Madison do most of the picking. He sat down at his desk and looked at Maxine.

"What?" Maxine asked.

"Nothing." Zachary paused. "Well, maybe something. I really like Madison. I don't know very much about her, but I really like her," Zachary stated, waiting for Maxine to start being nosy and ask him questions. She liked to jump to conclusions. Maxine looked at him and then said, "Zachary, you seem very happy right now. I don't know why, but if Madison has anything to do with it, then you definitely need to date her. You have everything that you want. You have a very successful company, and you have a beautiful home, and all you need now is a wife and lots of kids to fill it. So if you think that Madison might be that person, then go for it. But I'm telling you this: you are getting too old for fooling around, so if you're serious about this girl, you'll wait till marriage to sleep with her." Maxine sighed as she finished.

"I know you love me, Maxine. Thank you for worrying about me. I promise to be a good boy," Zachary answered, knowing that if Madison was the one. She was his soul mate.

* * *

Madison walked in her front door at six fifteen, later than she expected. She had a briefcase full of contracts and paperwork to go over, but right now all she wanted was a couple of Motrin, anything to soothe her nerves. She didn't want to have to sit down and think about Luke and how she was going to tell him that she wasn't interested. She didn't like this kind of conversation, but she couldn't get out of this. Madison retrieved her glass of water and her medicine and sat down in one of her leather, oversized chairs. She thought of Luke and how she felt about him. *That's just it,* she thought, *I don't think of him in that way.* She didn't know if she would. He was handsome and had money, but she didn't know if she could picture herself waking up beside him every morning for the rest of her life. And that's what she wanted; someone for the rest of her life. Madison got up and paced the room. At this very moment, she wished that she had a dog, something to shift her focus and something to take her mind off her worries and frustrations.

By the time midnight rolled around, Madison was still just as stressed as when Luke was in her conference room. "Lord," she prayed, "help me with my decision. Help me to know what to say. You know my future, and I don't think that Luke is the one. If he is, please show me." She decided that she had better go to bed and then get up early to start her day off right. She paused long enough to pick up the phone and wanted to call Zachary. She wanted to know if he had someone over there. After all, it was a Friday night. She wanted to know if he was home or if he was out. She dialed the first three numbers and then sat the phone back down in its cradle. She couldn't call him at this time of night; he would think she was stalking him. Madison walked back into her bedroom, looked at the phone again, sat down, stripped off her clothes, and then lay her head down on a pillow, where she fell asleep.

Zachary woke up feeling as if he were ten years younger. He couldn't remember the last time that he slept that well. He had fixed himself and Spanky a dinner consisting of pork chops and applesauce. They were one of Zachary's favorites. Then he grabbed Spanky and loaded up in the wrecker and ran a couple of accounts. He was home and in bed by eleven thirty. He enjoyed his life, but he was ready for something different; something to add a twist to his organized life.

He walked into the kitchen and poured himself some coffee and glanced at the clock; it read 10:18 A.M. *Wow*, he thought, *I actually slept in.* Sleeping in was not something that happened very often in his household. Spanky was actually still in bed snoring away. Zachary was going to call Madison, but he didn't want to wake her up, so he headed toward the bathroom and turned on the shower. He waited a full five minutes to get the temperature just right and then stripped and stepped into the hot water. Zachary looked across the bathroom into the mirror; *I still look good*, he thought. He had a nice six-pack across his abs, his arms were toned and tanned, and his legs were muscular. Every woman that he had dated had always told him that he had a great body. He leaned back into the hot water and started to wash his hair. He wondered what his life would be like when and if he ever got married, to have his house full of noise and stuff everywhere. He really thought he was ready to settle down, and to him, Madison was the one. "Lord, I pray that you guide me. Guide my heart and lead me to what is good for me. Amen," Zachary prayed in the shower. Twenty minutes later, Zachary stepped out of the shower feeling clean and relaxed. He quickly got dressed and went to the front door, opened it, and grabbed the newspaper. He went back to the kitchen table, threw the paper down, noticed Spanky by the back door, and let him out. Zachary sat back down at the table and started reading the paper, but his mind wasn't into it. He glanced at the clock. It read 11:31. *Okay,* he thought, *it's probably an acceptable time to call Madison now.* He reached over and picked up the phone and dialed her number by memory.

"Hello, it's Madison. I'm not available to answer the phone, so please leave a message after the beep," Madison's voice echoed. Zachary had a brief moment where he thought about hanging up but decided that she would have caller ID and she might think that he was weird if he hung up. So he decided to leave a message. He took a deep breath and said, "Hey, Madison, this is Zachary Mann. Just calling to say hi and to see if you had any extra time this weekend. Give me a call." Zachary smiled and hung up the phone. *Oh well,* he thought. *She's probably already gone or still sleeping.*

Madison heard the phone ringing but couldn't reach it. Her head ached, and she thought that she was going to be sick. She reached and grabbed her head, thinking that this would stop the spinning, but it didn't. All the stress had given her a headache and made her stomach turn. She crawled out of bed and barely reached the bathroom when she threw up. Madison thought that she was going to pass out right there on her navy blue bathmat. There was nothing in her system, but her nerves were so uptight anything was possible. She lay there for a good fifteen minutes. When she thought that she was well enough to get up, she went to see who called. *Probably just mom,* she thought as she wandered into the kitchen and hit her voicemail button.

Madison immediately felt better upon hearing Zachary's intoxicating voice. She smiled and replayed the message from Zachary. Should she call him? She thought that she should at least call him back to be courteous, but also because she wanted to talk to him. But first she was going to clean up, and the shower was calling her name. Forty-five minutes later, Madison emerged from her bathroom totally feeling good and dressed, ready for battle. She had enough time to think about what she was going to tell Luke, and she was ready to call Zachary and see what was on his mind. She walked through her living room, grabbed the phone, and walked to the back door. She opened the door and sat in one of the patio chairs. She had her phone, her glass of water, and she was ready to call him. *Mr. Mann,*

I hope you are the one, she thought. She dialed his phone number and waited. One ring, two rings...

"Hello?"

"Hi, it's Madison. I was just returning your call from this morning," Madison said and then bit her tongue, thinking that sounded dorky. "Did I catch you at a bad time?"

"No, I was just outside playing ball with Spanky. Thanks for calling me back. I was just wondering if you were available tomorrow for dinner." Zachary really didn't know what he was going to do, but the dinner invitation just popped out.

"Well, I think that I am. What time were you thinking?" Madison answered. She knew that she wanted to be with him, and she was just going to follow her heart, once she took care of the Luke problem.

"Tell you what, I'll just call you tomorrow and let you know the time. I think that we will go out to dinner to celebrate," Zachary responded.

"That sounds great, but to celebrate what?" Madison asked, wondering what Zachary was thinking.

"I just want to celebrate us getting to know each other and to decorating the house," Zachary said while rolling his eyes, thinking that was pushing the comfort zone with Madison and that he sounded like a dork.

"That sounds excellent. I'm really looking forward to dinner, Zachary. Thank you for asking. Tell you what, why don't you plan on coming over to my house first before dinner? We can visit a bit, and I think I might have some sample books here that we can look through. So I'll talk with you later tomorrow then," Madison responded. She couldn't believe her ears; he wanted to celebrate them. This was too perfect. She felt like this was a sign from God that they both wanted to get together. Maybe the feeling she had in her heart was the one that she was supposed to follow. Her heart led her to Zachary and no one else.

"Sounds great! Have a good day. Bye," Zachary said as he hung up the phone and sighed a sigh of relief. That conversation went so well. He knew that Madison was the one for him.

Madison hung up the phone and sat in her lawn chair, replaying the conversation that just took place. Was Zachary for real? Or was he just trying to get into her life enough to break her heart? Madison knew that she had enough heartache to last a lifetime, and she was ready to meet her soul mate. She walked back into the house and knew that she had better get to work on those contracts so she could prepare for tonight with Luke.

She sighed. How was she going to break it off with him? How was she going to be clear that she didn't want a relationship with him; that she didn't want more? How could she say this nicely but without anything missing? She had strong morals and had never dated two men at once. She didn't ever understand how anyone could do that. Her heart clearly told her now that Zachary was the one for her. She didn't want to string Luke along; she just had to tell him tonight that they could only be friends. She figured he would be mad, but she couldn't deny her feelings for Zachary any longer. Luke would just have to deal with the fact that they weren't meant to be.

"Luke, Luke, Luke," she said out loud as she went to the table to get the contracts out of her briefcase.

Madison was working on approving the contracts when she glanced down at her watch. It was already 3:00 P.M. She had to get up and around. She had to straighten up the house, decide what she and Luke were going to have for dinner, and then figure out when she was going to have the talk with him. Should it be after dinner, before dessert, or after dessert? She knew this was going to be hard, but she just hoped that she was making the right decision. She was stressed out already, and it wasn't even time to do any talking.

She got up and grabbed her car keys to run a couple of errands, dropping the contracts in the mail and swinging by the grocery store. She had decided on making lasagna with a salad tonight. She was a bit worried how Luke would react tonight. After all, he was coming over for dinner, and she figured that he was thinking it would lead to something more, but it wasn't. She just had to get the script down on how to let him down easy. She walked in the door of the grocery store. She was in the produce aisle when someone walked up behind her and gave her a hug. She spun around, scared that she wouldn't know who it was.

"Luke, what are you doing here?" Madison asked. How odd that she ran into him now when her thoughts were still on tonight and what she was going to do.

"Hey, Madison. I just came by to grab some groceries when I saw a perfect woman heading my direction. You demanded attention, so here I am," Luke said with a smile. He just wanted tonight to be amazing he wanted to have Madison in bed. That was his goal one way or another. He thought the roses were an extra touch. What woman didn't love roses?

"Luke, you're a goofball," Madison said halfway serious and halfway jokingly. "I was thinking of having lasagna and salad. What do you think?" Madison asked.

While Luke had been at home, one of his friends called and told him that he could borrow his plane whenever he wanted. Luke was considering asking Madison if she wanted to go to Las Vegas. He was hoping that maybe a little alcohol would make the evening a bit funnier. To make things a little more crazy, he called Mark to see what they had planned and to see if he and Abigail would like to go. Maybe Madison would want to go then, but he wasn't sure. He thought he would just surprise her with the trip. He didn't know exactly when he was going to ask her, but thought he might as well ask, since she was standing right in front of him. She was beautiful, and he couldn't wait any longer.

"That sounds great to me, but I have a better idea. I have a friend's plane sitting on the runway right now. What about taking off and going to Las Vegas for the evening? I've called Mark and Abigail, and they are meeting me there at 5:00 P.M. We can leave in about an hour and be home late tonight. What do you think?" Luke asked, wondering if Madison would go with him.

"Wow, that sounds like fun, but I don't think it's a good idea. Why don't we just stick to dinner like we planned? Madison replied.

Disappointed, Luke sighed. "Okay, if that's what you would like to do. Maybe we can go some other time."

"Maybe. I'll see you later tonight," Madison replied and went to finish her grocery shopping.

Madison left the grocery store, still wondering what she was going to tell Luke tonight. She had to figure it out quick because Luke would be over in about an hour or so. After putting all her groceries up and the lasagna in the oven, she walked down the hallway to her bedroom to get ready. What was she going to wear? She didn't want to look too dressed up but still wanted to look nice. She finally decided on a pair of jeans with a pink and navy striped shirt. *Not too dressy,* she thought. She had finished getting ready and went into the kitchen to make the salad and bread. Luke would be over shortly, and she really wanted to get this over with. Should she talk to him before dinner? Or after? She wasn't sure yet, she just figured that she would wait and see what his tone was. The doorbell rang, drawing her out of her thoughts, and she went to answer the door.

"Luke, you're right on time, come on in," she said with a tiny smile on her face. She didn't know when she was going to do this, but didn't feel like it would be right to wait all night before telling him things were over. But something stopped Madison in her tracks. There was Luke standing beside her, dressed up, and when she glanced behind him, a limo stood waiting.

"Luke, what's going on?" she asked worriedly.

"Well hello to you too," Luke answered and stood there waiting to be asked to come in. He was holding the bottle of champagne he had bought.

"Thanks for bringing the champagne. But I really want to know what a limo is doing outside my house," Madison replied, wanting to figure out what was going on. "I thought I would surprise you with a little trip. I thought we would go out for dinner, and I wanted to go in style. So just turn off the dinner, and let's go. Also, I wanted to talk to you about something," Luke said trying to get past her front door. "Have you made any decisions about our future and what you want from me?" Luke asked point blank.

Madison was frozen in place. Luke really thought that he was going to just show up with a limo and take her somewhere. Was he crazy? And on top of that he was already asking her what her decision was. He had already asked her earlier to go to Vegas with him, and she said no. Yet here he was with a limo. Did he not take a hint that she wasn't going anywhere with him? She looked up at him to reply, when something caught her attention. She glanced to the distraction, and it was a black and red wrecker truck with Mann Co. printed on the side. She just wanted to scream. She turned her eyes to see who was driving. Madison had no doubt in her mind that as Zachary had been driving by he ahd seen her standing on the porch with Luke glaring at her. He did have a vehicle on the back, so she didn't feel like he was stalking her. But still, what was he thinking?

"Hello? Madison? Are you okay?" Luke asked, still standing on the porch. "You look like you've just seen a ghost," Luke replied, getting more and more impatient.

Madison stood aside and said, "Yes, I'm fine. Come on in. I appreciate your offer for the trip, but I already told you earlier today that I don't think that is such a good idea. I don't know why you keep pushing the idea of us going somewhere tonight. I don't think it's a good idea. You asked me if I have made a decision, so I think we should discuss that first." She gathered her breath and wondered if she'd just lost her chance with Zachary. After all, she did have another man standing on her porch. Madison took the champagne out of Luke's hand, set it down on the counter, and then motioned for Luke to sit down on the couch. He did so with a smug look on his face. Did he know what was about to happen? *Oh well,* she thought, *I can't be worried about that. I must do this and then figure out what to do about Zachary.*

Madison took a deep breath and replied, "Well, I'm glad that you asked, because actually I do want to talk to you as well. I don't know exactly how to say this, but I just don't think this is going to work between us. You are a great guy, but I don't think that we are meant for each other. I want someone who believes the same way that I do. I want someone to spend the rest of my life with. I don't mean to hurt your feelings. I really thought that I could open up and fall in love with you. But it just isn't happening for me the way that I think falling in love should be.

You are a great guy—good looking, lots of money, and can really romance a woman, but I just don't think that I am that woman. I'm sorry if I hurt you. I really thought that we could have worked, but something is missing. I want it all. I want the fairy tale. I want the happy ending. I want to be totally and undeniably in love. I want my knees to get weak and my heart to miss a beat when I'm around the love of my life. But it doesn't all happen with us. I'm so sorry. So at this point, I don't think that going on any type of trip would be wise for either of us. I'm sorry." She finished, wondering what his response would be.

Luke just stared at her, not believing her words. She didn't want him? That was a shocker. "Well," Luke began, "I'm sorry that you feel that way. But honestly, I think you are making a big mistake. I don't think that you gave us a fair chance, but it doesn't matter now. If you don't mind, I think I'll just skip dinner. I don't want to be here anymore. I can let myself out," Luke announced, getting up and leaving without so much as a good-bye.

She could tell by the look on Luke's face that he was furious. He probably had never had a woman do this before. Most women would love to have him, but just not her. Madison went into the kitchen and turned off the oven. She didn't care if the lasagna burned; she had to talk to Zachary. She really didn't know what to do. Should she get in her car and go to his house? Should she just call him until he answered? She was upset and didn't have a clue on how to proceed from here. At the last minute, she called her mom and asked for her to come and pick her up. She was upset and needed a sounding board on what her next step should be.

Twenty minutes later, Megan was on Madison's porch ringing the door bell.

"Hi, Mom," Madison responded. "I'm glad you came over. I don't know what to do."

"Oh, honey," her mom began. "Whatever it is, we can get through this. Get your purse, and we'll go to the little diner up the road and get a piece of pie or a cookie," Megan finished, thinking that getting Madison out of her house would help. Madison grabbed her purse and locked the house up. She got into the passenger seat and just stared out the window. Megan didn't know why Madison called her over or what was going on, but thought that she should wait to start asking questions until they got to the diner. They had just settled down in a booth when the waitress walked up.

"What can I get the two of you? Honey, you okay?" she asked, glancing at Madison.

Madison looked up and smiled. "Yes, I'm fine. Can I get a Dr. Pepper and a chocolate chip cookie?" Madison answered.

"I'll just take a piece of chocolate cream pie and coffee," Megan replied, starting to worry about her daughter.

"It'll be right out," the waitress replied, and before she walked off, she said, "This is on the house, honey. You look like you deserve it."

Madison sat there, wondering what she was going to say to Zachary, should she ever get a chance to talk to him again.

Megan just looked at her, knowing that she would start talking when she was good and ready.

Madison had known both Luke and Zachary only six weeks but felt as though she had known Zachary her whole life. She wanted to see if there was something there. She had prayed about the whole thing, and she felt that Luke wasn't for her. He had made that pretty clear the way that he had been pressuring her to make a commitment before she was ready.

"Madison, are you okay? Talk to me," Megan pushed gently. Madison noticed that her cheeks were wet and reached up to wipe them away. She looked around and noticed that there were only a few people in the restaurant, and where they were sitting, in the back, there was no one around. She decided that she would tell her mom everything.

"I'm going to tell you, but don't interrupt until I'm finished, and please don't pass judgment." Madison paused to let all of that sink in.

"Okay, I'll just listen," Megan said, hoping that she wasn't going to hear something horrible.

"Okay, I'll start at the beginning. About six weeks ago, I was running late for work, and at a stoplight, I saw the most amazing man I had ever seen. Anyhow, I never thought I would see him again and agreed to go on a blind date with Abigail. She was setting me up with Luke. We all went to the Pelican Bar, and as we are sitting there, in walked the mystery man. He saw me, and I saw him. It was just crazy. Anyhow, shortly after that, Luke put all the pressure on me to commit to him, and I just couldn't. Then I went to teach the seminar, and guess who I ran into? The mystery man. Turns out his name is Zachary Mann, and he owns a repossession company. He has hired me to remodel his home for him, and I am actually looking forward to it. Anyhow, I have been praying that God would give me a sign about what I am supposed to do and who could possibly be my soul mate. Everything points to Zachary. When I told you I had a breakfast appointment with a client, it was Zachary. Yes, most of it was business, but the most amazing part was that he prayed before we ate. It was just amazing, and I really feel like I can act myself with him. We have a lot in common, one being our faith.

Then tonight, Luke showed up to dinner, where I was going to end things. But he pulled up in a limo thinking that he was going to take me on some kind of special trip. As I was standing there, Zachary drove by, and I know he saw me with Luke. I'm really worried that Zachary thinks there is something more with me and Luke, and that is not correct. Needless to say, I think Zachary is really upset with me, and I told Luke that I couldn't go with him and that I didn't think he was the one. That is why I'm sitting here now," Madison said and noticed that a tear was rolling down her face.

"Oh, sweetheart, why didn't you talk to me in the beginning?" Megan asked, so concerned that her daughter was going through this and there was nothing that she could do. "You have got to go with your heart and not worry about anything else. You know that you have prayed over the situation and that God will lead you through this, but it sounds like you already know what you need to do. Why don't you call Zachary, and I will take you over to his house?" Megan pushed gently.

"Okay, I'm ready. Thank you for coming and getting me, and thank you for not judging me. I'll have enough of that when Abigail gets home," Madison replied, picking up her cell phone to call Zachary. She thought she remembered his number but wanted to be sure, so she started digging around in her purse for the piece of paper that she had written it on. Madison opened her phone and started dialing Zachary's phone number.

"Hello?" Zachary answered, trying to juggle driving and answering the phone.

"Zachary. Hi, it's Madison. I know that you're probably wondering why I'm calling, but I really need to talk to you. Are you home? If not, what time will you be home? I'll come over. I just need to talk to you," Madison said, thinking that she was going to make a complete fool of herself.

"Hi. I'm surprised to be hearing from you tonight. You looked pretty busy when I drove by," Zachary answered, upset with himself for sounding disappointed.

"I'm sorry, really. Will you just give me a chance to explain? Please?"

"Well, I'm pretty busy, but I would like to hear what your story is. I should be home in about twenty minutes. I just need to run by the office and drop off this vehicle," Zachary finished, sounding a bit disheartened.

"Okay, I'll see you soon," Madison replied and hung up.

"Okay, Mom will you take me over there? Zachary will be home in about twenty minutes, and it will take us about fifteen to drive over there, give or take, so I can wait for him. That will give me time to think about what I am going to say." They both got out of the booth and headed out the door.

Fifteen minutes later, Megan pulled up to Zachary's house. Madison noticed that Zachary wasn't home yet, which was fine with her. She would just sit on the porch and wait.

"Thank you for driving me here. I'll be fine. Zachary will be here at any time, and besides, I need to think about what I'm going to say. Thanks, Mom. Love you," Madison said as she reached over and gave Megan a quick kiss and hug and got out of the car.

Megan pulled off. She was worried about Madison but knew that she was a grown woman and knew exactly what she was getting into.

Ten minutes later, Madison saw a truck turn down the street, and sure enough, it was Zachary's. She stood up and tried to smooth down her hair and clothes and started walking toward the truck. She was stepping out in faith, and she had to go with her heart.

Zachary was shocked to see Madison waiting on him and thought that she had bad news to tell him. He didn't know what to expect. He pulled in the driveway and headed up to the porch.

"Hi," Zachary said and paused, not knowing what was going to come next. "You look a little stressed. Let's go inside," Zachary said as he unlocked the door and held it open for Madison.

Zachary held the door and slowly led her inside and sat her down on the sofa.

"What's going on, Madison? Talk to me," Zachary asked, probing a bit much even for his taste.

"Well, where do I begin?" Madison paused, only scared that Zachary didn't have the same feelings, but she had to try, and began her story. "Okay, first I have to say that I'm so sorry about earlier tonight. The man you saw on my porch was Luke. I have only known Luke for the last few weeks, and we have been on a couple of dates. Luke has been putting pressure on me to make a commitment to him, but I knew that I didn't want that. See, I had seen the most beautiful man one morning at a stoplight. I didn't think that I would ever see him again, but I did. He walked into the same restaurant that I was in one night, and then I ran into him again at the design conference.

"Luke was supposed to come over tonight, and I had planned on telling him that we didn't belong together and that I couldn't see him anymore. Well, he changed the plans to take me on a trip, so that's why he showed up in a limo. But I didn't know this and didn't want to go anywhere with him. I was going to tell him that we didn't belong together anyhow. So I did tell him how I felt, and then he left. When I saw you drive by, it was like it was a sign, and I knew what I needed to do. I had to talk to you. I know what I want, and I know what I deserve. I deserve a Christian man; I deserve to be loved and to be in love. I want to feel butterflies in my belly every time I talk to the man I love. I want it all, and I want that with you. But one thing that I don't know is if you have a girlfriend or if you're involved in a relationship. If you are, I will gladly leave right now and leave things as they are. But I knew that I had to try and tell you how I feel or I would never forgive myself." Madison paused, thinking that he was going to tell her that he was involved with someone and that she would have to leave brokenhearted.

"I don't know what to say." Zachary paused, wondering how this could be happening to him. He had been praying for a sign, and look what was sitting on his sofa, his sign. Madison felt the bottom of her stomach give out and thought she might throw up her chocolate chip cookie. Zachary looked at her and smiled. "Madison, where have you been all my life? I knew that I wanted to meet you from the first day I saw you at the stoplight. I just didn't know how. Then we saw each other again at the restaurant and then again at the design conference. Something kept pulling us together, and I believe that God had a huge part in this. I'm not seeing anyone except my work. I didn't know what to think when I saw Luke on your porch this evening. I thought my world was going to stop, but something deep within me said to be patient. I am relieved that you finally have made your decision. I'm just thankful that it ended this way for us. I think that we belong together, and I want to see where this goes. I believe in God and the signs that He gives us, and I would say that He gave us both one tonight," Zachary answered as he smiled and shifted over on the couch until he was in arms reach of Madison.

Madison smiled and closed the space between them and looked up, making eye contact. He reached out and stroked her cheek, wishing to take care of her and to never let anything happen to her. Madison smiled against his hand, thankful she went on faith and told him exactly how she felt. Zachary gently placed his hand behind her neck and pulled her into the most intimate kiss she had ever had. Her hands automatically went around his neck and tightened the embrace and passionate kiss they shared. The fireworks were going off in her mind and stomach. *This is what falling in love should feel like,* she thought. She never wanted the kiss to end, and neither did Zachary. He continued to kiss her and then finally ended their first kiss. He looked at her with a smile and laughed. "Well, that is a first kiss to go down in the record books." Smiling, he pulled her into a hug. "But, you have to prove yourself," he said, pausing. "First things first—I have to see if you can make it in my world. Let's go repo a car." Zachary finished laughing. Madison looked at him and started laughing as well. "Okay, Mr. Mann, I'll show you what I'm made of. Let's go."

Madison couldn't believe this. He wasn't seeing anyone, and now he was seeing her, and she was going to repo a car. Madison started laughing and knew this was going to be one night that she would never forget.

8

The next six months went by so fast that neither Madison nor Zachary barely had time to look up. Madison had been busy on the weekends and the evenings at Zachary's house, remodeling the house as well as keeping up with the busy demands of her company. Trent Design was growing by leaps and bounds, and Madison finally had to break down and hire an additional ten staff members just to help carry the load. They had completed the project for Dylan and Noah, and it was a huge success. Dylan and Noah had loved the work so much that they were sending referrals to Madison, not to mention all the calls from the design conference that were still coming in. Madison had never been busier or happier.

Zachary was completely the same. The repossession company was booming, and he was looking to expand the company's lot to hold more vehicles as they were brought in. Life was so good for Zachary. He had the love of his life, and his business was really doing well. What more could he ask for? He only had one more thing to do and that was to ask Madison to marry him. He had met Megan several times over the last six months, as well as Abigail, although Abigail didn't take to him as fast as Megan did, but she was coming around. Zachary's parents just loved Madison, and they were so thankful that Zachary had met a nice Christian woman. Madison went to church with Zachary as much as she could with her schedule. Everything was working out. Zachary thought of the perfect evening to propose. He picked up the phone and called Trent Design.

"Good afternoon, Trent Design. This is Sandi," Sandi answered smoothly.

"Hello. May I speak to Megan, please?" Zachary asked.

"Yes, hold just a moment while I transfer you to her," Sandi replied and transferred the call.

"Hello, this is Megan."

"Hi, Megan. This is Zachary, but before you say anything, can you talk privately?" Zachary asked. He didn't want Madison to be in the same room.

"Yes, I can talk. What's up?" Megan asked. She absolutely loved Zachary; he was a perfect match for her daughter.

"I would like to invite you over tomorrow night for dinner. Madison doesn't know anything about this, and I want it to be a surprise. I will invite my parents over as well, so when you get there they will be waiting to let you in. I will go and pick up Madison and bring her to the house. Can you be there around six?" Zachary asked.

"Yes, that sounds great. Why the secret?" Megan asked, wondering what was going on.

"Well, that is another thing that I would like to talk to you about. Can you get away for a couple of hours for lunch today?" Zachary asked, hoping that she could.

"Let me check my schedule. The only thing I was supposed to do was to go over some contracts with Madison, but I can get out of that. Where and what time do you want me to meet you?" Megan asked, really getting excited that this could be huge—whatever it was.

"Let's say twelve thirty, and let's meet at Teala's. I'll see you in just a little bit," Zachary stated and was smiling as he set down the phone.

Megan set down the phone. Could this be the time? Could Zachary be planning to propose to Madison? "Don't get your hopes up," Megan told herself. She checked her watch; it was already eleven thirty. She had to figure out a way to get out of her meeting with Madison. She decided to go into Madison's office and think on the fly. After all, she had to leave to meet Zachary on time. She walked into Madison's office and noticed that she was daydreaming.

"Hi, Madison. What are you up to?" Megan asked, hoping that Madison couldn't see that she was up to something.

"Nothing really. I mean, I have a lot of work to do, but it's Friday, and I'm tired and excited. My whole life has changed in the last few months, and it is just great. I can't wait to see Zachary this weekend. I called to see if he wanted to have lunch, but he said that he was busy and couldn't," Madison said looking a bit disappointed. "I haven't talked to Abigail in over two weeks, and that has me a bit bummed. I think that she is still upset with me about the whole Luke thing. I can't say I blame her, but I wish that she would understand." "I have an idea," Megan said. "We were supposed to meet to look over contracts, but why don't you go get Abigail, take her to lunch, and make her talk to you?" Megan suggested. "It would probably do both of you some good." She hoped that would be enough to get her out of the meeting.

"Are you sure you don't mind?" Madison said, looking up at her mom.

"Absolutely, honey. Just go and enjoy your afternoon. I can take care of things here," Megan stated.

"Okay, that sounds good. I will go and get Abigail and drag her out of her office if I have to. I might not be back, but just call me if you need me," Madison stated as she put the papers in her desk and started getting her purse and keys.

"See you Monday," Madison said as she walked out the door.

"See you, honey," Megan answered, thankful that she had gotten out of that. Now all she had to do was to wait for Madison to get in her car and leave. She knew that Abigail and the restaurant that she was meeting Zachary at were on the opposite sides of town, so the odds of running into each other were slim. She waited for ten minutes and then left to meet Zachary.

Zachary didn't know the last time he had been so excited. Madison had called and asked him to lunch, and he felt horrible that he couldn't make it, but he did have a good excuse; he was having lunch with her mom to ask for Madison's hand in marriage. This was going to be a great weekend. Zachary had arrived at the restaurant with about ten minutes to spare and got a table toward the back. He always had a habit of sitting where he could see everyone; he didn't like his back to the door. Right on time, Megan came rushing in. "Sorry, I'm late," Megan said as she gave Zachary a hug.

"You're not late; you are right on time," Zachary replied.

For the first time ever, Zachary was a ball of nerves. Here he was sitting with Megan, about to ask for her daughter's hand in marriage and for her help in picking out the ring. He had never been so nervous.

"Okay, I know we have been making small talk, but I want to talk about something important, and I need your help." Zachary paused, waiting for Megan's reaction. But Megan's face was calm with a flash of excitement.

"Whatever I can help with, I will. Is something wrong?" Megan asked, suddenly worried.

"No, nothing like that. Megan, I love your daughter. I have loved her from the first time I laid eyes on her at the stoplight. I know that she is a gift from God and that He brought us together. I promise that I will take care of her and love her and support her. If it is all right with you, I would like to propose to Madison tomorrow night at the cookout." Zachary paused, waiting for Megan's response.

Megan tried to maintain her composure as tears flowed down her face. "Oh, Zachary, of course you can ask Madison to marry you. You are a great man of God, and I couldn't ask for any more. Nor could I ask for anyone else to take care of my little girl for the rest of her life. I know that her dad would have loved you, and you have my blessing," Megan finished with fresh tears rolling down her face.

"Thank you. I plan on asking her tomorrow night after dinner," Zachary replied just as their lunch showed up. For the next forty-five minutes, they ate and talked about Zachary's plans and where he thought they would want to get married.

"Oh, one more thing I need your help with," Zachary asked. "I need your help picking out Madison's engagement ring. I have a pretty good idea of what I want to get. I just want your opinion on it," Zachary finished.

"I would be honored," Megan responded.

After they ate lunch, Zachary suggested they go to the jewelry store, which was just a couple of blocks away. Megan agreed and suggested that they walk. The afternoon was beautiful. They walked, both in their own worlds—Zachary thinking of just how he was going to propose, Megan thinking of the wedding planning that soon would be underway.

They looked around the jewelry store for about an hour, and then Zachary found what he was looking for. Megan was shocked; Zachary was holding a perfectly shaped, two carat, pear diamond. It was exquisite. Madison was going to love it. Zachary looked at the salesperson and simply stated that he would take it. Megan was thankful that his business was doing so well; after all, he just paid in full for Madison's engagement ring. Megan knew that Zachary could take care of her daughter and treat her like a lady. That impressed her. She thought back to her late husband and knew that he would be happy as well that Madison had met someone who had the same beliefs and would take care of her forever.

The next afternoon, Zachary thought he had everything in order. His parents were coming over at five, Megan coming over at six, and everything was going to be perfect. He had the steaks marinating and the potatoes cleaned and ready to bake. The salad was already prepared. The only thing he didn't know about was the dessert. He had asked his mom to take care of that. The house remodeling was complete. Zachary had really just let Madison do what she felt would look right, and she had great taste. The house had never looked better. Right at five, the door opened, and in walked Zachary's parents, Jake and Carol. Zachary always had a great relationship with his parents, and he couldn't wait to tell them the news as well. Carol had made dessert, and Zachary wasn't sure what it was, but it looked delicious.

"Mom, what did you make?" Zachary asked curiously. Spanky was already in the kitchen, sniffing everything out.

"Oh, that. I just threw some Cherry Delight together, nothing big. But I hope you like it. You had mentioned on the phone that you needed to talk to us and something about Madison and her mom coming over. What is going on?" Carol asked and eyed her son carefully.

"Well, Mom and Dad, why don't you sit down before Megan gets here?" Zachary paused, waiting for them to sit down at the kitchen table. When they were settled, he continued, "The reason that I asked all of you here tonight is that I plan on proposing to Madison, and I wanted you here because you are a very important part of my life," Zachary finished, wondering what was going on in his parents' minds. He didn't have to wait long to find out.

"Oh my goodness! Oh, Zachary!" Carol shouted and leaped up and embraced her son in a huge hug. "I am so happy for you. We absolutely love Madison. She is an exceptional woman, a woman full of faith, and I think you two will be amazing together," Carol stated.

"Congratulations, son," Jake said, also giving his son a hug. "Just remember to keep Christ first and everything else will follow suit. Marriage is hard, but if you work together, everything will be fine," Jake finished, feeling himself getting a little sentimental.

"Thank you both so much for being so supportive. Everything I've learned about marriage, I have learned from watching you. You both have kept your faith strong over the years, and that is what I want and need for Madison and I," Zachary stated and gave them both a bear hug. Just then the doorbell rang.

"That is Megan," Zachary said while walking toward the door to open it.

"Hi," Megan said as she walked in. Zachary made the introductions, and all three parents sat down and were talking about wedding plans. After twenty minutes of that, Zachary asked his dad to start the grill and that he would run and pick up Madison. He didn't want Madison to drive herself over, in case she was early and saw her mom's car in the driveway. Besides, he wanted a little alone time before the family time came.

Another twenty minutes later Zachary was pulling into Madison's driveway to pick her up. The only thing Madison knew was that she was going over to Zachary's to have dinner with his parents. She didn't suspect a thing. Zachary made small talk with Madison, talking about their weeks and trying not to sound too excited about tonight. Madison was just chatting about work as they turned onto Zachary's street.

"Here we are, sweetheart," Zachary said while opening up the door for Madison to get out.

"Thank you, honey," Madison said while standing on her toes to give Zachary a kiss before they went in to have dinner with his parents.

Zachary opened the front door, and Madison walked in. She heard two female voices in the kitchen and knew one of those was Carol's, and the second seemed like ... *Oh no,* she thought. *What's my mom doing here?* She turned and looked to Zachary for an explanation.

"Surprise! I invited your mom too. I thought we could all sit down and have dinner. Since we are a couple now, I thought it was time that our parents met," Zachary said while taking her hand and pulling her into the kitchen.

Jake was busy outside grilling the steaks and potatoes, and the women were in the kitchen getting all the sides ready. *This seems so right,* Zachary thought. "Thank you, Lord," he said to himself.

Over the next two hours, the families ate and visited and caught up on one another's lives. It was a very comfortable and relaxing atmosphere. Madison was enjoying it immensely and then noticed that Zachary had gone into the kitchen with Carol but really didn't give it much thought. She just figured they were getting a drink or something. When they returned, Carol sat down by Megan, and they started talking. Then Zachary came back into the room and sat down beside Madison, took her hand, and looked up. Everyone got quiet. *What's going on?* Madison thought. She was soon going to find out.

"Madison, there is a reason why I asked for both of our parents to be here tonight. I wanted this to be special. Madison, I love you with all my heart. You are an amazing woman, and I want to spend the rest of my life with you." Zachary paused, letting all of this sink in. Madison was sitting there, wondering if this was going where she thought.

"And," Zachary continued, "I promise to love you every day, to help you succeed and become whatever you want to be. I promise to keep Christ first in our relationship and to obey the Word of God. I promise to never go to bed upset with you or us angry at each other. I have loved you from the moment I saw you and have wanted nothing else since. Madison"—Zachary got down on one knee and continued to hold her hand—"will you give me the honor and privilege of marrying me?" Zachary asked.

Madison looked at the man of her dreams, and looked at her mom, and her in-laws-to-be and thought, *This is how it is supposed to feel, completely right.* She knew as well that they belonged together for the rest of their lives. "Thank you, Lord," she said to herself and looked at Zachary, placing her hands on his hands.

"Zachary, I love you. You are a great man, and I would love the honor to be your wife. Yes, yes, yes!" Madison squealed. Zachary pulled out the ring, and Madison was honored and shocked at the size of it. She was officially engaged to Mr. Zachary Mann—the man she had been holding out for: Mr. Right.

.

Lightning Source UK Ltd.
Milton Keynes UK
UKOW04f2141110216

268195UK00001B/98/P